SNOOPING CAN BE

Doggone Deadly

SNOOPING CAN BE
Doggone Deadly

LINDA HUDSON HOAGLAND

Jan-Carol
Publishing, Inc
"every story needs a book"

SNOOPING CAN BE DOGGONE DEADLY

LINDA HUDSON HOAGLAND

Published November 2014
Little Creek Books
Imprint of Jan-Carol Publishing, Inc
All rights reserved
Copyright © 2014 by Linda Hudson Hoagland

ISBN: 978-1-939289-55-1
Library of Congress Control Number: 2014958375

You may contact the publisher:
Jan-Carol Publishing, Inc
PO Box 701
Johnson City, TN 37605
publisher@jancarolpublishing.com
jancarolpublishing.com

This book is dedicated to my family:
Mike, Sherry, Matt, and Becky

Dear Reader

Lindsay Harris tries to live a normal life. That is a life as close to a normal that a single mother of a set of teenage, twin daughters and a preteen son can live. As in your life and mine, things happen.

Lindsay has no control of accidental events that happen to her family which has grown by one to add her newspaper friend, Jed.

I was a legal assistant/secretary in my distant past, but I never ran into all of the troubles Lindsay and group have faced for which I will be eternally grateful.

In the fourth volume of Lindsay's trials and tribulations, you can read about the disappearance of Emily, Jed's car accident, and the vanishing of the parents of Annie's neighbor; as well as the reason for the death of a dog that they are trying to ascertain.

The answers can only prove that SNOOPING CAN BE DOGGONE DEADLY.

Yours truly,

Linda Hudson Hoagland

Acknowledgments

As always, Janie C. Jessee, my publisher, garners my heart-felt thanks for allowing me to do what I most like to do: write.

Thanks to Tammy Robinson Smith for asking me to start this little series and the encouragement I get from her to continue.

Thanks to all of those writers who have allowed me to be their friend. You all know who you are.

Chapter 1

"Annie, have you gotten yourself a new dog yet?" I asked as I walked into her office. She was the receptionist at the law office where I spent my days working as a legal assistant/secretary. The title really depended on Wayne Maxwell's mood that specific day.

"No, I looked at some, but it is so hard to replace my Harvey. I'd had him since he was a tiny puppy and I was in junior high school. He was the love of my life," she said as she fought back the tears that appeared every time she talked about her beloved dog who had been a mutt, a mixture of the breeds from the neighborhood.

"Don't you think it's about time you found a new love?" I asked in an effort to cheer her up a little.

"I'm afraid the same thing that happened to Harvey will happen to a new dog," Annie said sadly.

"Did you ever find out how Harvey died?" I asked with concern etched in my voice.

"No and that's the problem. Someone killed him and I don't have any idea why," Annie explained.

"You thought it was your neighbor who killed him. Do you still think that?" I probed.

"Yes, but I have no way to prove it. He still isn't very friendly, but it's like he is ashamed or hiding something," Annie said.

"I'm going to make it my next project. First to find you a new love, the perfect dog, and second to discover why Harvey was murdered," I said with conviction.

"How are you going to do that? He was my dog and I couldn't find out anything," asked Annie skeptically.

"I don't know yet, but I will find out what happened to Harvey. You can be sure of that, Annie," I said with assurance.

"Okay, but I don't see how. I didn't get a necropsy, an animal autopsy, done because I couldn't afford it. There is no way we could prove anybody outright killed Harvey. Most people I have talked with thought he died of natural causes," said Annie.

"You really don't believe that, do you?" I asked.

"No, I'm sure somebody killed him," said a determined Annie.

"When can we go look for a new dog, Annie?" I asked enthusiastically.

"What about Saturday morning?" said Annie with an equal amount of enthusiasm.

The happiness that returned to Annie's face made me smile inside and out.

"I might have my kids with me, but I will pick you up at nine o'clock and we will go dog hunting. If my kids see all of the dogs and cats at the shelter, I'm afraid I will have to get one for my house, too," I said as I shrugged my shoulders in submission.

"That's not a bad thing," said Annie.

"No, it's not. It is just an extra responsibility for mom ... me," I answered.

Chapter 2

I still had to finish a Deed of Trust for a local bank, so I wandered back into my tiny office so I could finish typing the detailed entry of the lengthy property description.

The trip into Annie's office to talk with her about her dog, a diversion for me because the tedious input onto the Deed of Trust of numbers and directions, such as east, west, north, and south, was getting on my nerves at the time.

I started working on the keyboard again, but I found my mind wandering back to the dog. There had to be a reason that someone had killed Annie's dog.

Drugs killed a number of humans. Maybe they had also caused the demise of Harvey, Annie's dog.

Of course, there could be an altogether different reason or maybe he had died of natural causes. He had been getting older, after all. I didn't think that this was the case, though. I thought Annie's dog had been murdered.

I picked up my telephone and started dialing the number for the town police. I had a friend or two on the force who might be able to help me get started by giving me a little background research on Annie's neighbor, the suspect in Harvey's murder.

"Town police," said a strong male voice.

"May I speak with the chief? This is Lindsay Harris calling," I said in an almost whisper. I didn't want Wayne to hear anything I was going to ask the chief.

"One moment please, Ms. Harris," he said politely.

"Lindsay, what can I do for you?" asked a cheerful Brian Hope, the Chief of Police for the Town of Stillwell.

"This is nothing for Wayne. This is something I'm checking into for some answers for Annie," I explained.

"Okay, what is it?" asked Brian.

"We think Annie's neighbor killed her dog, Harvey. The neighbor acts suspicious around Annie, unfriendly like," I explained.

"Give me some information on him—name, address, etc.—and I'll check him out," said Brian as he tried to end the conversation.

"Okay, I'll call you back after I get it from Annie. Talk to you later, Brian," I said as I hung up the receiver.

Brian didn't really sound that excited about getting involved in my little investigation, but that was fine with me.

I glanced at the clock and realized it was almost lunchtime. I hurried out to Annie's office to get the information I needed before she left for lunch.

"Annie, can I ask you a couple of questions?" I whispered conspiratorially.

'Sure, what do you need?" Annie said with a smile that totally lit up her face.

"I need your neighbor's name, address, phone number, and any other information you might have about him," I whispered.

"Why?" Annie asked.

"I'm having the police check him out for me. My thought is that he might be into drugs. What do you think?" I asked Annie.

"You can do that?" Annie asked.

"Not officially. The police officer is just doing me a favor," I explained without naming names.

Annie began to write the answers to my request for information onto a notepad. When she was finished, she ripped off the small page of paper and handed it to me.

I snatched it from her and hurried back to my office to call Brian again.

Chapter 3

"May I speak with Brian?" I asked the female voice that answered the police department phone. The phone clicked as my call was placed on hold.

I stared at the small note I held in my hand that contained the information I was going to read to Brian.

DENNIS MARTIN
302 St. Albans Road
Stillwell, VA
276-555-1212

I glanced at my watch and realized it was time for me to relieve Annie so she could go to lunch.

I disconnected my phone call, then grabbed my notepad and a couple of folders so I could look busy if Wayne decided to check on me while I sat at Annie's desk to field incoming phone calls and drop-in visitors.

Wayne had no appointments scheduled for the day so if we had visitors, they were not expected.

Never the less, I had to man the front desk just in case—Wayne's rule.

I spread out my folders, scrambled the papers a bit, and pulled my notepad to the top of the pile where I had attached the information I had attained from Annie.

I dialed the town police number again.

"Hello, this is Lindsay Harris. May I speak with the chief? I called earlier but I had to hang up," I explained, hoping the chief was not upset because I'd had to disconnect my previous call before we had gotten an opportunity to speak with each other.

"I'll check. Hold on, please," he said professionally.

The front door opened and in walked a young man dressed in blue jeans and an old, but clean, tee shirt.

"May I help you?" I asked as I continued to hold the phone close to my ear.

"Yeah, I need to talk to a lawyer," he said in a whisper.

"What is the problem?" I asked as I tried to get enough information from him to determine if it was a case that Wayne would want. Usually, whatever case Wayne didn't want to bother with was funneled to Everett for disposal. Wayne got first dibs since his name headlined the letterhead.

"It's my parents," he said softly.

"What about your parents?" I asked.

"I don't know where they are. They are supposed to be visiting my aunt in Florida. But they aren't there. I don't know what to do," he said as he tried to be manly and show no emotion. I could see the tears forming and beginning to flood his eyes.

"Attorney Maxwell is not in the office at the moment but Attorney Everett Barton might be available. Have a seat and I'll ask if he has the time to see you," I said as I pointed to a chair in which I wanted him to sit while I walked back to Everett's office.

"What is your name?" I asked before leaving the room.

"Dennis Martin."

7

Chapter 4

My mouth flew open but I had enough common sense to close it before I made a fool of myself.

I turned abruptly and walked, no ran, to Everett's office.

Everett's door was standing open like always, so all I had to do was speak to get his attention.

"Everett, we have a walk-in who needs some help. Would you want to talk with him?" I asked in a barely audible tone.

"What's his problem?" asked Everett loudly, making it obvious that he wanted me to add a little volume to my words.

"He can't find his parents. He says they are missing. The funny thing about this whole situation is that he is also Annie's neighbor. She thinks he killed her dog," I explained softly so my voice wouldn't carry to the front office.

"Really?" Everett said as he nodded. "Send him back. I'll make sure I close the door. I don't want Annie to know he is in here until I hear his story."

I left Everett's office to fetch Mr. Dennis Martin. I led him back to Everett's office and I closed the door softly. By the time I returned to the receptionist desk, the phone call that had placed on hold had been disconnected again and I was getting a dial tone when I placed the receiver to my ear.

"Darn, now I know the chief is really going to be angry with me," I mumbled.

I heard the door open again and there stood Annie.

"Anything happen while I was gone?" she asked with a smile.

"Just a walk-in who is now talking with Everett," I said without giving any details.

"Is it an interesting case?" Annie asked.

"I think so," I said as I gathered my folders and papers so I could return them to my office.

I wasn't sure what I was going to do. If Everett took Dennis Martin's case, I would be able to get all of the information I could ever need about Dennis Martin and might be able to find out if he killed Annie's dog if I was able to look through the case file.

I couldn't call the police chief again to ask him to check out Annie's neighbor because there was a possibility he could become Everett's client. That little stunt wouldn't be too cool on my part as Everett's legal assistant. Everett didn't have a problem with my title like Wayne did.

How would I tell Annie about her neighbor if Everett took the case?

Chapter 5

I ate my lunch at my desk to save some money. My children, bless their little souls, needed extra money this week that I hadn't set aside in my budget. Schools, with their clubs and activities, always seemed to have their hands out ready to receive your hard-earned cash.

My intercom buzzed and when I answered it, I was surprised to hear Everett's voice.

"Lindsay, call Annie into your office and close the door. I will be in to talk to both of you after you get her in there," said Everett.

"Sure," I said as I disconnected from Everett and punched Annie's number.

"Annie, I need you to come back here and help me with something. It'll only take a couple of minutes. Don't worry about the front desk. There shouldn't be a problem," I said, lying through my teeth.

"Be right there," she said, and I soon heard her heels clicking down the hallway.

I sprang from my desk as soon as I saw her enter the room and rapidly closed the door behind her. A few seconds later, Everett walked past my closed door, talking in hushed tones to someone.

The bell attached to the front door tinkled and Annie sprang up from the chair in front of my desk.

"Sit, Annie, that was Everett," I said.

"What's going on?" asked Annie.

"I don't really know, but I think we are going to find out now," I said as my office door was opened by Everett.

"What's up?" asked Annie.

"We have a new client, Annie, and I wanted you to know who he is and why I am taking his case," Everett said with sincerity.

"Who is it?" asked Annie curiously.

"His name is Dennis Martin, your neighbor," Everett answered softly as he watched her reaction.

"Why would you do that?" Annie demanded.

"He needs someone to help him," said Everett in a soothing tone.

"What is his problem?" Annie snapped.

"His parents are missing. He needs help holding off the creditors so they don't try to take the house," explained Everett.

"Oh," groaned Annie.

"I hope it doesn't create a problem for you," said Everett.

"No, sir, no problem," said Annie as she glanced at her feet. There is one thing I would like to know."

"What's that?" asked Everett.

"Did he come here because I work here?" asked Annie as she looked directly at Everett.

"Yes," replied Everett with no further explanation.

The bell above the front door tinkled again and Annie charged out of the room to check on the visitor.

"What is the problem that Annie has with Dennis Martin?" asked Everett, closing my office door once Annie had left the room.

"I told you earlier that she thinks he killed her dog," I said softly.

11

"Did he?" Everett asked.

"That was what she and I were going to try to find out before he walked through the door. We were going to find the answer to that question," I told Everett.

"How were you going to do that?" Everett asked.

"I don't know yet, but I thought it was about time she found out if he killed her dog or not," I said forcefully.

"Okay, okay, Lindsay, I will try to find out for you guys. Will that satisfy you?" asked Everett.

"Yes," I answered as he walked out of my office.

Chapter 6

At five o'clock I raced out the door to pick up my girls to take them to drama club and to drop my son, Ryan, off at the YMCA to meet his friends for basketball practice.

After they each exited the car, I drove to the house to start dinner for all of us. It would be a late dinner, but they didn't seem to mind. I was sure they had snacked at the house before I had picked them up.

My children were growing up and forming their own friendships and relationships with others, leaving me out in the cold. That was something they were supposed to do whether I liked it or not.

I was going to have to spread my wings a little and seek a relationship that was not made up of family.

Having endured a bad marriage and ugly divorce several years earlier, I had been hesitant about forming new ties for fear they, too, might be broken.

A working mother with three very active kids, I found it hard to form new bonds. There just didn't seem to be the time available for that kind of pursuit. I had a best friend, Marni, but she didn't have children, so our lives had led us in different directions.

I had been thinking about someone in particular recently. My brain told me to avoid the flights of fancy, but my heart ached for me to take a chance.

My cell phone rang and pulled me out of my daydreams.

"Hello," I said hesitantly.

"Lindsay?"

"Yes, who is this?" I asked.

"Jed."

"What's wrong, Jed?" I asked as I tried to figure out why I didn't recognize his voice or his phone number, which flashed on my identification pad.

"I was at a friend's house and I have been involved in a little accident," he explained.

"Okay, go on," I said worriedly.

"Well, I was actually in your neck of the woods checking on some missing people when some lunatic ran me off the road and I hit a fence and crashed on through a corn field," Jed said.

"Who did that to you?" I asked as my mind went to the missing people and Dennis Martin.

"I didn't actually see who it was. I just caught a glimpse of the driver and I didn't recognize him," Jed said.

"Who were the missing people?" I asked.

"The Martins. They have been missing for a few months. Their kid reported them as missing recently. Seems they had been out of town to visit relatives, so he really doesn't know how long they have been gone," he continued.

"Yeah, I know," I said softly.

"How do you know?" asked Jed.

"As of today, the kid is a Everett's client," I answered. "Now, back to you. Where are you?"

"At the hospital. Can you come pick me up? When I get to your house, I'll call someone in Bristol and see if they can give me a ride home," he said in a pleading tone.

Chapter 7

I glanced at my watch and decided that I had enough time to gather Jed up, take him to the house, then go get my kids from drama club and the "Y."

I pulled up to the patient loading area in front of the hospital, left my car running, and ran inside to find Jed. I spotted him in a wheelchair with a pretty young hospital volunteer standing beside him and listening attentively to his every word.

It suddenly occurred to me, at that point in time, how strikingly handsome Jed was. It wasn't that I had not noticed his appearance before, because I most certainly had. What caused this surprising realization was the fact that others thought the same thing.

I waved at Jed to get his attention.

"Hey, Lindsay, I'll be right there," he said as the young lady started pushing Jed and wheelchair toward me.

My mouth dropped open when I saw he had a cast on his left leg, and then saw metal crutches leaning against the wall that were obviously meant to accompany him when he left the hospital.

"You didn't tell me you broke your leg!" I said as I gathered up the crutches. "My car is parked right out front."

The volunteer pushed the wheelchair through the automatic doors and waited for me to open the car door to allow Jed to climb into the front passenger seat.

I pushed the seat back as far as it would go so that Jed could stretch out both legs, especially the one in the cast.

When we were both settled, and after he had dismissed the little lady helper, I started my barrage of questions.

"Did you break anything else?" I asked as I started the car. I knew my tone was sarcastic, but that was fine with me.

"No, that's the only bone," he mumbled.

"Good," I said a little more gently.

"What did the police have to say?" I asked.

"They filed a report and will look into it," Jed answered. "I believe it will probably be filed away forever and ever. I did ask them for a copy of the police report so that I could send it to my insurance company. Maybe the insurance company can get them to do something, especially since I think my car was totaled."

"Nothing else is broken, but did you do any other kind of damage?" I asked.

"I have just a few cuts and bruises. I banged the back of my head pretty hard. It didn't break the skin, but I have a good-sized knot back there," he said as he rubbed his head.

"You could have been killed, Jed," I whispered.

"Yes, ma'am, I could have, but I wasn't. Not this time anyway," he said.

"Do you think there will be a next time?" I asked.

"Yes, I do," he said softly.

"Why?" I asked.

"I asked the wrong person a question. That's the only thing I can think of. I think it was related to that boy's missing parents," he explained.

"You mean Dennis Martin?" I asked.

"Yes," he said.

16

I arrived at my driveway, where I parked as close to the house as I could manage. It would be easiest for him to go into my house through the front door. There weren't as many steps to climb.

I helped him into the house and parked him on the sofa. I had to hurry so I wouldn't be late gathering my girls, Emily and Ellen, along with Ryan, my son.

Chapter 8

I found my girls standing in front of the school talking to some friends who were also waiting for their parents to drive them home.

"Mom, I think I get to play the lead in the play," said Ellen, bubbling over with excitement.

"What play?" I asked.

"It's one that the teacher wrote about bullying. I really like the play and I love the part," she gushed.

"What about you, Emily? Did you get a part to play?" I asked my quiet daughter.

"No, I didn't try out," she said sullenly.

"Why not?" I asked.

"I didn't want to, that's all," Emily snapped.

"Ellen, go inside the "Y" and tell your brother to come on," I said to Ellen, trying to get her to settle down a bit.

"It's Emily's turn, Mom. She is supposed to do it this time," she argued.

"Okay, okay. Emily, go get your brother so we can go home and eat supper," I said sternly.

"Oh, all right," she said as she slammed the car door.

"What's wrong with your sister?" I asked Ellen.

"I don't know. She wouldn't tell me," answered Ellen.

Ryan and Emily came running to the car to climb in for the ride home. Emily sat in the front seat next to me and remained quiet. Ryan sat next to Ellen and he, too, was quiet, but for a different reason from Emily. Ryan was tired from physical activity.

"Guys," I said, as I maneuvered the car onto the driveway, "Jed is inside and he has a broken leg. I had to go pick him up at the hospital because his car is wrecked."

"Is he okay?" asked Ryan. "That means he can't take me fishing, doesn't it?"

"Well, he can't right now, but he will. He promised. Jed keeps his promises," I said soothingly.

"Is he going to stay with us?" asked Ellen.

"I don't know. I haven't asked him yet. I wanted to know that it was okay with you guys," I answered.

"Where will he sleep?" asked Emily. It was the first time she had opened her mouth since returning to the car with Ryan.

"I was going to let him have my room. I can sleep on the sofa," I answered after a slight pause to figure out what to say.

"Ryan has an extra bed in his room. Why can't he sleep in there?" asked Emily.

"Because I haven't asked Ryan. If Ryan doesn't want to share his room with Jed, I'm not going to make him do so."

"No, I don't want to share. He can use your room, Mom," said Ryan.

"No problem, Ryan," I said with a smile. I had known that would happen. Ryan would have had to have cleaned up his room in order for Jed to stay in there.

We entered the house to find Jed sleeping soundly.

"Sh-sh-sh," I said as I held up my finger to my lips.

Ryan entered the room, followed by Ellen. Before Emily reached the doorway, I touched her arm to get her attention. She turned to look at me.

"We need to talk," I whispered.

Emily continued into the room and then walked to the hallway that led to her bedroom. I closed the door, locked it, and then stood outside of Emily's door, prepared to knock. Emily pulled the door open before my knuckles reached the door panel and said, "What?"

"What's wrong?" I asked as I pushed my way into her room so I could close the door.

"Nothing, Mom. Absolutely nothing is wrong," Emily said, her voice breaking. I could hear the tears threatening to break through.

I reached out and pulled her close to me. I held her and gently squeezed her to let her know that I was there no matter what the problem could be.

Emily crumbled into tears and I would not let go of my sobbing daughter. When the tears lessened I asked, "Emily, tell me what is bothering you."

"I can't. You will think I am so silly," she said between intakes of breath.

"No, no, never, Emily. I love you so much," I said in a soothing tone.

"Ellen stole my boyfriend right out of my life," she blurted out in a loud, harsh whisper.

"Boyfriend? I didn't know you had a boyfriend," I said as I continued to hold her and gently stroke her back.

"I know, but I really did like Raymond. She sashayed herself right up to him and took him for herself," she sniffled angrily.

"If he really liked you, she wouldn't have been able to do that, you know," I said softly. "Don't waste your time and tears on him. He isn't worth it."

"Aw, Mom," she said as she cried some more.

"Em, get ready for bed and sleep on what I told you. When you get up in the morning things will be better. I promise you that tomorrow will be a better day," I said as I kissed her on the cheek, released her from my embrace, and left her room, closing the door softly behind me.

Chapter 9

I yawned as I walked into my room. After I changed the sheets on my bed, I would chase Jed out of the living room. I would be able to sleep more comfortably on the sofa than Jed would, especially since he had a broken, cast-covered leg to contend with. As I finished putting on the new sheets, I snagged a pillow and blanket so that I would have something to sleep with, and then headed into the living room.

"Jed, I need you to wake up so you can walk to the bedroom for me," I whispered into his ear.

"Hunh? What?" he mumbled as he fought the effects of the drugs that had been administered to him in the hospital.

"You need to stand and lean on me so I can get you into bed," I said.

"What? Lindsay?" he said as he opened his eyes.

"Come on, get up," I urged.

Finally, I could see reality fill his brain and force his eyes to focus.

"No, Linds, I should go home," he said loudly.

"Sh-sh-sh," I said. "I hope the kids are going to sleep. It's too late to drive you home. Besides, I don't think you should be alone tonight."

"No, no, I'll be fine. I'll just call my buddy, Mike, to come pick me up," Jed said in a truly unconvincing tone.

"I've cleared it with my kids, Jed. You can stay the night, but I need for you to sleep on my bed and I will sleep on the living room sofa. Come on now. I'll help you get settled, then I will go crash on the sofa."

"Okay, Linds," he whispered. "I promise to go home tomorrow."

It was a struggle to get him to the bedroom, but getting his blue jeans off his body over the cast was an even greater struggle.

Eventually we both collapsed onto the bed in laughter.

I jumped up off the bed and looked at Jed. As much as I wanted to stay on that bed next to Jed for the night, I knew it wasn't going to happen. Not tonight.

"Jed, you're going to have to finish undressing yourself. I'm going to go to the living room to get myself ready for bed. I have to go to work tomorrow and then I will drive you home if you think you can take care of yourself. If you don't think you will be able to get around well enough, you can gather up some clothes and stay here with us until you are able," I said as I exited my bedroom, leaving Jed to sleep in my cozy, comfortable bed that I would surely miss as I endured a night on the sofa. The things you do for your friends can truly be amazing.

I knew that Jed's visit would be hard on me emotionally because I was beginning to enjoy his company way too much. I wasn't ready for that leap of faith.

I walked into the living room, spread out my blanket, grabbed my pillow, and tried to make myself comfortable.

I was in one of those wide-eyed states when, no matter what, I was not going to be able to sleep for a while.

23

Jed was awakening feelings in me that I thought I had buried after my ugly divorce from Justin, the father of my children.

I wasn't prepared for the emotional roller coaster that I knew was ahead of me.

Chapter 10

I tossed, turned, and struggled with my blanket and pillow until I finally fell asleep due to pure exhaustion.

It was not a restful sleep.

I dreamed.

A big dog came running after me, chasing me, and growling like he was going to chew me up. When he got close enough to bite me, his image faded and suddenly I was running from a dark figure without a face.

I wanted to turn around so I could see the face of the dark figure, but in order to do that I would have to slow down. He would catch me if I slowed my pace. He might catch me anyway, no matter what I did.

This is a dream, right? I can slow down in a dream. It doesn't matter if he catches up to me. It is only a dream.

I stopped running and spun around to look head-on at the figure chasing me.

I woke up screaming.

Ryan came running into the living room, asking, "Mom, are you okay?"

I finally got my wits about me and I answered, "Just a bad dream. I am fine."

"What were you dreaming about?" Ryan asked.

"Someone was chasing me, but I couldn't see who it was," I explained.

"Do you want to come and sleep in my room?" Ryan asked with boyish sincerity.

"No, baby, I'll go back to sleep right here. I'm sure I won't be bothered by that bad dream again," I answered with a smile. "Were you awake already when I screamed?"

"Yeah, something woke me up but I couldn't figure out what it was, and then you screamed. I was scared for a second, but I came out to check on you anyway," he explained.

"I'm so sorry I scared you. I'm surprised your sisters didn't wake up and run in here," I said.

"I guess they didn't hear you," Ryan said.

"You go back to bed, Ryan. I'm going to check on your sisters and then I'll go back to sleep," I said softly.

I walked down the hallway in the silence of an almost sleeping house. Hopefully Ryan and I had been the only ones rambling through the rooms at two in the morning.

When I reached the door to my bedroom, I cracked it a tiny bit and saw Jed totally asleep and sprawled out on my bed. I closed the door softly and walked on to Ellen's room where I found her peacefully asleep.

The next room was Emily's and I truly hoped she was asleep and not fretting over the lost love.

I tapped softly on Emily's closed door and waited for a few seconds for an answer. I could hear her moving around making rustling noises.

I tapped softly again and called out her name.

"Emily," I said, my voice a little above a whisper.

"Go away," she whispered harshly.

I pushed open the door and stood facing her.

"Why are you awake?" I asked.

"I couldn't sleep. My mind was wide awake," she said angrily.

"Forget about that boy, Emily. Ellen probably talked to him to make you mad," I said.

"Well, it worked. I am mad and I'm going to get even with her," she growled.

"How are you going to do that?" I demanded.

"Forget it, Mom. I'm just running off at the mouth. I won't do anything," she said apologetically.

"Do you promise, Emily?" I asked.

"Good night, Mom. I'm going to go to sleep now," Emily said sweetly.

I turned to leave, and then realized that she hadn't promised me that she would not get even with Ellen. I shook my head, dismissing the thought, and walked to my sofa where I would try to sleep until the alarm would ring in less than four hours.

Teenage drama was a bit too much at two in the morning.

Chapter 11

At 6 a.m., my alarm jolted me out of a deep sleep. I jumped up, raced to the bathroom, and threw cold water onto my face.

I needed to get the kids up so they could get ready for school. My morning ritual was to knock on each bedroom door until I heard an answer from each occupant.

"Ryan, get up," I shouted.

"Okay," he said sleepily.

"Ellen, time to get up," I shouted.

"Aw, Mom, I want to go back to sleep," Ellen said.

"You can't. Now move it," I growled.

"Emily, let's go," I said as I stood outside of her bedroom door. Her usual response was 'I'm up' but I didn't hear it this time.

"Em, it's getting late," I shouted a little louder.

No answer.

I opened the bedroom door and saw an empty, unmade bed. I walked through her room and opened the bathroom door that joined Emily and Ellen's bedrooms.

"Mom, what do you need?" said a surprised Ellen.

"Where is your sister?" I asked.

"I don't know. She is usually up and dressed before me, but I didn't see her," explained Ellen.

"What happened yesterday between you and Emily?" I asked as I watched for her reaction.

"What are you talking about?" asked Ellen.

"Did you talk to Emily's boyfriend?" I asked.

"What boyfriend?" Ellen asked, confusion clouding her face.

"Emily said you stole her boyfriend," I explained.

"Again, what boyfriend? If she likes someone, I always steer clear and she does the same for me," Ellen explained.

"You saw her last night. What happened to cause her to be in such a bad mood?" I probed.

"I don't have any idea, Mom. She was like that when we went to drama club," said Ellen.

"Okay, okay. I will go check the rest of the house to see if I can find her," I said as I turned to leave.

"You want some help?" Ellen asked.

"No, you just get ready for school. I'll make sure your brother is getting ready, too," I said, then I knocked at Ryan's door.

"Are you up, Ryan?" I shouted.

"Now I am," he said.

I hurried to the kitchen; no Emily.

I saw a note laying on the table.

Mom,
I walked to Maddie's house. I will get a ride to school with her.
Love,
Emily

"Maddie? Who is Maddie?" I mumbled.

I placed bowls, spoons, cereal, and sugar on the table so Ryan and Ellen could help themselves. I went to the fridge for the juice and milk before I put on a pot of coffee for myself and my house guest, Jed.

When Ellen appeared in the kitchen, I immediately started with the questions.

"Who is Maddie?" I asked point blank.

"I don't know a Maddie," Ellen responded.

"Is there a new girl in any of your classes?" I asked.

"No—wait a minute—yeah, there is, but I don't know her name," she answered with hesitation.

"Did your sister talk to her?" I asked.

"I don't know. We don't always hang out together. She's been so moody lately," said Ellen as she shrugged.

"When did all of this happen?" I asked.

"All of what?" asked Ellen.

"The moodiness, the fact that you two aren't close like you used to be," I said.

"About a month ago," said Ellen.

"Why?" I asked.

"I really don't know, Mom," Ellen answered.

"Eat your breakfast. The bus will be here soon. I need to check on your brother," I said as I left the kitchen.

"Ryan, how's it going?" I shouted as I opened his bedroom door.

"I'll be right there," he said as he grabbed his backpack.

"Go eat your breakfast," I said as I left his door open and went to knock on my bedroom door.

"Yeah," said Jed.

"I need to get some clothes so I can get ready for work," I explained.

"Come on in," he said cheerfully.

I opened the door and saw him sitting on the side of the bed. He had managed to get his jeans on but his shirt remained unbuttoned.

I gathered what I needed and headed for Ellen's and Emily's bathroom, hanging my clothes in there until I came back to take my shower.

I glanced at the clock in Ellen's room and raced to the kitchen to get Ryan and Ellen out the door to catch the bus.

"Ellen, tell your sister to go to the office and to call me when you get to school," I instructed.

"This really proves that we both need a cell phone," said Ellen.

"Me, too," chimed Ryan.

"Not now, both of you," I snapped.

"What if I don't see her?" Ellen asked.

"Then you call me, okay?" I said as I tried to hide my irritation.

"Ryan, do you know Maddie?" I asked him as he raced passed me.

"Yeah, she lives about a mile from here," he shouted as he ran to the bus.

I wanted to question him some more, but the school bus door closed and whisked Ryan and Ellen away to school

I could not understand why Ryan knew Maddie but Ellen did not know her.

I ran back inside the house and shouted to Jed, "I'm going to take a shower. There's coffee in the kitchen."

I emerged from the bathroom off of Emily's bedroom freshly scrubbed, wide awake, and dressed for work.

In the kitchen sat Jed as he munched on a bowl of cereal and sipped some coffee.

"Thanks for letting me crash here, Lindsay," he said as he tried to force a smile to his face.

"Leg hurting?" I asked when I saw him wince.

"A bit," he said as he winced again.

"You can stay here if you need to," I said.

"Thanks, but I need some clothes, so I had better go home," he explained.

"Okay, but how are you going to get there?" I asked.

"I'll make a couple of calls and see if I can get someone to pick me up," Jed said. "It's okay if I use your phone, isn't it? My cell phone battery is dead."

"Sure, but if you can't find anyone, I'll drive you home when I get back from work," I said. "You can use my phone all you want."

"Good, while I'm waiting for my ride, if I get one, I'll make some calls about the missing parents of Dennis Martin."

"Will you tell me what you find out?" I asked.

"Sure. You go on to work and I'll call you if I can get a ride or not," said Jed as he waved me out the door.

Chapter 12

Life is getting complicated again, I mused as I drove to work.

Emily was suffering, but I didn't know why. I hadn't noticed a change in her mood. If I had, I would have chalked it up to her monthly cycle. It always made me moody, so maybe Emily had inherited my problem.

Moodiness rarely seemed to be a problem for Ellen. Her mood remained on an even keel most of the time.

Jed was another complication I had not expected to crop up in my life as a single mother. I shook my head as I tried to dismiss the thoughts of Jed.

When I pulled into the parking lot at work, Annie was waiting for me. She didn't like to go inside the empty building all alone.

Annie had her keys out, so she unlocked the door and we entered the building with a great deal of noise designed to scare away any unwanted visitors.

"Annie, I may be getting several personal calls today. My friend, Jed, is at my house and he will probably call me," I said hurriedly, hoping she would not want me to explain more.

"At your house? Did he stay the night?" she asked as she smiled broadly.

"Yes, but it is not what you think. He was in a car accident yesterday and broke his leg. He needed a ride and I didn't think he should be alone, because he was pretty drugged up," I explained.

"Oh, is he okay?" Annie asked.

"I think so. He is supposed to call me later and let me know if he can get a ride," I answered.

"Okay, no problem. Who else? You said several calls," said Annie.

"Either Emily or Ellen will call me. I don't know which one or maybe both of them will call. I just don't know," I said with exasperation.

"Is there a problem?" asked Annie.

"I don't know. I'll find out when one or the other of my daughters calls me," I said as I threw my hands in the air to fight off the anger that was building up inside of me.

Annie read my body language and didn't ask me any more questions.

I entered my office and spread the papers that I needed to work on out before me. I did most of Wayne's real estate work, which I found totally boring, but it was a living.

I began to enter a large, tedious property description into the computer, but was interrupted when my intercom burped and Annie announced that I had a call on Line 1. Apprehension filled me as I picked up the receiver.

"Mom?"

"Ellen?"

"Emily's not here. She didn't come to school," Ellen said excitedly. "Where is she?"

"I don't know, but I plan to find out. I love you. You go on to class and I'll talk to you after school," I said sternly.

Ellen disconnected and I placed a call to the school and asked to speak with Ryan, declaring that it was an emergency. I waited for such along time that I thought they had forgotten about me.

"Hello?" said a young male voice into the phone.

"Ryan, it's mom. I can't find Emily. You said you know who Maddie is. Emily left a note saying she was going to Maddie's. What is Maddie's last name? Where does she live?" I asked.

"I don't know her last name and I don't know which house she lives in, but she gets on the bus about ten stops from our house," Ryan explained.

"Okay, honey. You go back to class. I'll see you when we get home. I love you," I said as I hung up, fighting the urge to scream.

I gathered up all of the papers on my desk. I turned off my computer, grabbed my handbag, and walked toward Annie's office to tell her I had to go find my missing Emily.

"Call me as soon as you can and let me know that she is okay," said Annie. "I'll let Wayne know that you had a family emergency."

"Don't tell him the reason, okay, Annie?" I said as I ran out the door.

Chapter 13

I had forgotten all about Jed and his dilemma until my cell phone chirped.

"Hello?" I said as I struggled with the phone while I was driving.

"Lindsay, what's wrong?" he asked. "When I called your office, Annie said you had to leave because of a family emergency."

"Hold on, I'm going to pull over to the side of the road so I can talk," I said as I maneuvered the car to the graveled edge.

"Are you okay?" asked Jed.

"No, I'm not. I can't find Emily. She left me a note this morning saying she was going to Maddie's and then to school," I said in a flurry of words. "I don't know a Maddie. Emily's not at school. I'm so worried," I said as I fought to hold back tears of angry frustration.

"Calm down, Linds. Teenagers can be a pain," he said in a soothing tone. "You've left work; now where are you headed?"

"To the school. Ryan said there is a Maddie who lives about ten stops beyond our stop on the school bus route. That puts her pretty close to the county line, I think. I'll find out where she lives from the principal," I explained.

"Good. Call me as soon as you find out anything," he said as he disconnected the call.

I drove on to the school. I needed some answers and I was hoping they could give them to me.

"I'm here to see Mrs. Webber," I told the young lady at the front counter in the school office. "My name is Lindsay Harris and it's about my daughter, Emily."

"I'll go tell Mrs. Webber that you are waiting," the young lady said as she walked hurriedly away from the counter.

I didn't have to wait long before Mrs. Webber appeared at the counter with her hand extended in greeting.

"What can I do for you, Mrs. Harris?" she asked me.

"My daughter, Emily, is missing. She left the house early this morning, leaving a note saying she was going to Maddie's house and then to school. I don't know Maddie. I don't know where she lives, but my son says she lives about ten stops from our house. Can you tell me who Maddie is?" I said as I struggled to keep myself from bursting into tears.

"Who is your daughter's bus driver?" Mrs. Webber asked.

"Dan Perkins," I answered.

"Excuse me a minute while I call the Transportation Department to ask them," Mrs. Webber said as she started pushing numbers into her phone.

I listened as she held an extended conversation with the secretary of the Transportation Department.

"Her name is Madelyn 'Maddie' Stevens. She lives at 1432 Barnes Road. She didn't come to school today either," said Mrs. Webber.

I wrote the address down on the notepad I had fished out of my handbag.

"Thanks, Mrs. Webber. I hope to be able to send Emily back to school tomorrow. In the meantime, I will go visit Maddie Stevens," I said as I left the principal's office.

I climbed into my car and started driving towards Barnes Road.

My cell phone rang and I pulled over to the curb to answer it.

"Lindsay?" said a whisper on the other end of the line.

"Hello? Who is this?" I asked.

"It's Jed. There is something going on at the house next door. There are two cop cars out front and they have their guns out like they are going to shoot someone. Who would the police be after next door?"

"I don't know. There is an elderly couple living there," I said.

"I'm going to sit right by the window and watch what is happening. Where are you headed now?" asked Jed.

"I'm going to find Maddie Stevens. The principal gave me the address. I hope to be home in a little while with Emily in tow. In the meantime, you find out what's going on next door," I said as I disconnected the line to Jed.

Chapter 14

I had to drive passed Annie's house to get to Barnes Road and the Stevens house. I glanced at the house next to Annie's and saw Dennis Martin peeking out his front window before he quickly closed the blinds. It seemed really strange that his blinds were still closed, since it was only about ten in the morning. He should be leaving the blinds open to let in the light of the day.

I wondered who he was afraid of and why?

I drove on a little bit further to the address Mrs. Webber had given me. I pulled over to the side of the road to park. Then I thought that maybe I should call Jed and tell him where I would be, just in case.

"Jed, I'm at 1432 Barnes Road," I said as soon as Jed answered the phone. "I don't expect any trouble, but I wanted someone to know where I would be, just in case. Oh, by the way, my phone charger is in the kitchen if you want to plug in your cell."

"Just in case of what?" he asked.

"Just in case, that's all. 1432 Barnes Road. Write that down," I said sternly, and then I disconnected the call and climbed out of the car.

I walked slowly up the walk as I intently watched the front door of the house for any kind of movement.

I knocked hard so the sound could be heard anywhere inside the house. There was a strange echo, an empty house echo, that came back to me after I finished the knocking.

No one answered my knocks, so I pounded hard with my closed fist.

Still, no one opened the door.

I decided to walk around to the back of the house. Maybe someone was outside of the house and hadn't heard me pounding on the door.

I shuffled through the tall grass. It looked like the yard hadn't been mowed for a couple of weeks.

When I reached the back of the house, there was nothing there. There were no outbuildings or a garage.

The windows of the back of the house were bare. There were no curtains or drapes covering the windows. I walked up to those bare windows and peeked inside the room that was completely bare of furniture. Obviously, the house was unoccupied.

Now what?

I went back to my car to sit down for a minute to think about my next step.

I checked out the houses on each side of 1432 Barnes Road. There were cars in each of the driveways. I needed to go talk to the neighbors.

I approached the house on the left side with trepidation. I knocked a couple of times before a lady finally came to the door.

"Hi, I'm Lindsay Harris and I'm looking for your neighbor, Maddie Stevens. Has she moved?" I asked.

"That house is empty next door and has been for several months. The people that lived there were named Hudson. The mister found a better job in Cleveland, Ohio. He packed up the family and moved there. The house had been for sale for quite a while," the neighbor explained.

"You've never heard of Maddie Stevens?" I asked.

"No, I can't say that I have," said the lady as she stepped away to close the door.

I walked back to my car where I paused for a moment before going to visit the neighbor on the right side of 1432 Barnes Road. The door opened before I had a chance to knock.

"May I help you?" asked the sinister looking man at the door.

"I'm trying to locate your neighbor, Maddie Stevens," I said as I stepped away from the opened door.

"I don't know no Maddie Stevens," he said. "Do you want to come in?"

"No, no thank you. Maddie Stevens had given the address of the empty house next door as her address. Did a young lady about ten to fourteen years old live there?" I probed.

"No, I don't think so. Come on in and we will talk about it," he said with a glint in his dark eyes that scared me.

"No thanks, I'm trying to find my daughter who is supposed to be with Maddie Stevens," I said as I ran to my car.

I climbed onto the front seat and locked the car doors.

That man truly scared me. I hoped Emily didn't run into him. I was afraid to think of what could have happened.

I glanced at Dennis Martin's house as I drove home. The blinds were still drawn and he was not letting any of the outside world enter his house.

I pulled into my driveway and I was approached by a police officer.

"Who are you?" he asked without any kind of preamble.

"Lindsay Harris. I live here," I answered.

"Go inside and stay there. Make sure everything is locked up tight," he instructed.

"Why?" I asked.

"There has been a prison escape and we believe one of the prisoners is headed here to see his friend, who lives next door to you," he explained.

"I'm sorry, but I will be in and out. As a matter of fact, I was going to call the police because my daughter, Emily, is missing," I said in a tone that was just as stern as his own.

"Don't call. I will take the info from you and get it out to everyone. Just give me a few minutes to get someone to cover for me," he said as he turned to walk to his police vehicle.

I went inside the house where I expected to see Jed waiting for me next to the window.

"Jed, where are you?" I shouted when I didn't see him.

"In here," came a weak answer.

I walked to my bedroom and found him lying on my bed.

"Are you okay?" I asked.

"I don't feel well, Linds. I think I have some kind of infection. Did you find Emily?" he asked weakly.

"No, I didn't. I'm going to call an ambulance so you can go back to the hospital," I said as I touched his feverish head.

"No, no, I need to stay and help you find Emily," he said.

"You're too sick, Jed. You really need some medical help. I'll find Emily. When I do, she will be grounded for the rest of her life," I said as I dialed 9-1-1.

When the ambulance pulled into my driveway, the policeman came running.

"What's going on?" asked the stern-sounding officer who I had spoken with when I arrived home.

"My friend is sick. He needs to go to the emergency room. You never did come back to talk with me about my missing daughter," I said accusingly.

"No, ma'am, I was waiting for my relief to get here. He is running late," he explained.

The paramedics burst through the door, pushing a gurney as fast as they could.

The police officer glanced at Jed, who obviously wasn't the escaped prisoner, and then motioned for the paramedics to load him up.

I shouted, "Jed, I'll come to the E.R. as soon as I can. I need to report Emily as missing,"

I was near tears again. I didn't know what to do next, other than sit down and sob.

While my best friend was being loaded into the ambulance, another police car pulled up in front of the house next door. The police officer who had been waiting for his relief suddenly appeared at my side.

"What is your daughter's name?" he asked.

"Emily Harris. She is fourteen years old and she is an identical twin to Ellen Harris. I saw her last night at about two in the morning when I awoke from a bad dream and decided to check on my daughters. She was still awake, so I told her to try to get some sleep. When I checked this morning and found her bed empty, I started looking for her and found a note," I said as I handed the note to the officer.

"Who is this Maddie?" he asked after reading the note.

"I don't know. I went to the school to find her address. When I checked it out, it was an empty house. I'm really worried about Emily," I said as I fought the tears again.

"I need a recent photograph. Would she have gone to another friend's house?" asked the officer.

"No, I don't think so. She would have put that in her note," I explained.

"Would she have run away?" he asked softly, knowing the question would upset me.

"No, she has no reason to run away," I sputtered,

43

"I'm going to get this info out on the radio. You should call some of her friends after school is out for the day. They might be able to tell you something," he suggested.

"Okay," I said.

"There will be some detectives here later to ask you some more questions. You need to stay here in case your daughter tries to contact you," said the police officer in consoling tones.

He was gone, and suddenly my house was devoid of people. I sat on the sofa, wide-eyed as I tried to figure out my next step.

I called Annie.

"I can't find Emily," I whispered to Annie through a tear-constricted voice.

"I'll come over as soon as I get off work. I want to tell you what's happening with Dennis Martin in your absence," she whispered conspiratorially.

"Okay, I'll be here," I said.

Chapter 15

I sat in silence until Ellen and Ryan came bursting through the front door after the school bus had dropped them off.

"Did you find Emily?" asked Ellen.

"No," I answered.

"Where could she be?" Ellen asked.

"I was hoping you could help me with that," I said.

"How?" Ellen asked.

"Who are Emily's friends? Are they the same friends that you have?" I asked Ellen.

"Some are, but I don't really know who her close friends are now," explained Ellen.

"Why?" I pleaded.

"She changed. She didn't like anyone any more, Mom. Didn't you notice? It was so obvious," Ellen explained.

"Why didn't you tell me?" I asked Ellen.

"I didn't think I needed to do that," whined Ellen.

"Okay, okay. Can you tell me any of the names so I can give each of them a call? Maybe one of them has seen Emily," I said.

"I'll go write them down for you, Mom. She'll be home soon. I'm sure of it," said Ellen as she tried to console me.

While Ellen was making me a list, I called the hospital to check on Jed.

"Hello, my friend, Jed, was delivered to the emergency room by ambulance a couple of hours ago. Could you tell me how he is doing?" I asked.

"One moment, I'll transfer you to emergency," said the professional-sounding voice as she clicked off abruptly.

There was a hello from the harried nurse and I repeated my requested.

"Are you a relative?" asked the nurse.

"Yes, I'm his sister, Lindsay," I lied, knowing full well that they would not tell me anything unless I was a family member.

"Yes, he said you would be calling. He is being admitted. He has an infection around the break. He is not in a room yet, so you'll need to call back in about an hour and he will be able to talk to you from him room phone," explained the nurse.

"Okay," I said, then I disconnected the line.

I sat there on the sofa, staring at nothing. I was completely unfocused and my mind was racing as it searched for answers I couldn't find.

"Mom, Mom, what's the matter with you?" asked Ellen as she shook me gently.

I turned my face toward Ellen, but I was still not focusing.

"Mom, what's wrong?" asked Ellen in a louder voice.

I shook my head from side to side. I guess I thought it would shake me out of my trance-like state I had to come back to reality whether I wanted to or not.

"I'm okay, Ellen. I was just thinking," I explained.

"Here's the list of phone numbers of our friends. I don't know who her new friends are," said Ellen as she handed me the long list.

"Ellen, get my cell phone and start calling some of those people. It's in the kitchen hooked up to the charger. I'll call from the house phone. We need to speak to everyone we can," I said to my worried daughter.

"What should I say?" Ellen asked.

"The truth. Tell them you're trying to find Emily. That's all you need to say," I instructed.

When Ellen and I both finished the list of names, we had discovered nothing that would help us find Emily. No one seemed to know anything about Madelyn 'Maddie' Stevens, the new girl in town. I didn't buy that for a minute. If Emily had met her, I was sure some of the others in their circle of friends had met Maddie Stevens and just weren't talking.

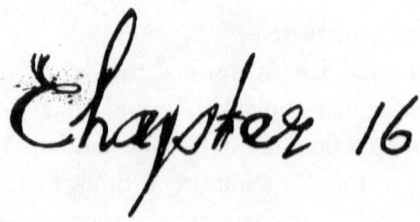

Chapter 16

My spinning mind finally stopped on Jed. I had to check on him. I dialed the hospital number and was greeted by a cheerful voice asking how she could help me.

"Jed Thompson, please. He was admitted today," I said solemnly, unable to make myself sound cheerful.

"He is in Room 325. I will ring that number," she said politely and I heard the rings begin.

After the fifth ring, Jed answered with a drowsy hello.

"How are you doing?" I asked as cheerfully as I could muster.

"Hurting. My leg is hurting really bad. It's a staph infection," he mumbled.

"What do you need for me to do for you?" I asked, expressing heartfelt concern.

"Let me sleep. It doesn't hurt so much if I sleep," he slurred.

"I'll come see you tomorrow, Jed. Just go to sleep," I said as I disconnected the line.

"Well, he's okay for the night. That's one worry tucked away for a few hours," I said as I took a deep breath and exhaled slowly.

"Ryan, tell me about Maddie Stevens," I said to my son when he entered the room.

"Like what?" he asked.

"What do you know about her?" I probed.

"Not much. She rides our school bus sometimes. She doesn't ride it every day, so I guess she misses school a lot," he said, shrugging his shoulders for emphasis.

"Have you heard anything, anything at all, that can help us find Emily?" I asked my young son.

"No. I know her name and where she gets off of the school bus. I've heard that she is a little strange," Ryan said.

"Strange? How strange?" I asked.

"She just doesn't act like the other girls. You know what I mean," he sputtered.

"No, I don't know what you mean," I said, trying not to let my agitation show.

"Well, Mom, she doesn't act like Ellen and Emily. Maddie acts more like you," he said.

"You mean she is older or that she acts older," I said.

"Yeah, that's it," said Ryan.

My mind went to the place where I would never want my kids to live: the street. That alone didn't make Maddie a bad person. It only pointed out the fact that she had to do what it took to survive.

If Maddie was a street child, I wanted to meet her, to help her, to let her know that she wasn't alone in this world.

If there was another reason for Maddie to be so different that my young son would notice it, I wanted to know why.

'No news was good news' was a stupid phrase to hear when I was waiting for word about finding my long lost daughter. Hopefully that was all it was: Emily was lost, not kidnapped, not raped, not murdered and never coming home again.

I walked out of my front door and approached the police car parked out in front of my neighbor's house.

The policeman saw me approaching and waved at me so he could speak with me.

"Ma'am, where are you going?" he asked sternly.

"I was looking for you. Something occurred to me while I was sitting in my house waiting for news about my missing daughter," I explained slowly.

"What was that, ma'am?" asked the police officer.

"Maybe, just maybe, my daughter is missing because of this escaped prisoner you are looking for," I continued slowly and clearly.

"How is that?" asked in the interested police officer.

"Maybe the prisoner arrived at my neighbor's house before you guys arrived here. Just maybe my daughter, Emily, walked out the back door at the same time he arrived. And, maybe, he had to take her with him to keep from being discovered," I said as I glanced at my feet for reassurance and then looked directly at the police officer to see if he might display a flicker of hope that this explanation could be plausible.

The police officer sat silently. The sound of the radio was the only noise coming from the unmarked police vehicle.

"Well, what about it? Do you think it could have happened like that?" I asked as my anger was starting to erupt.

Chapter 17

The police officer looked at me as if he were seeing me for the first time.

"What time did you say your daughter left home?" he asked excitedly.

"I really don't know. She was still here at 2 a.m. because I talked with her at that time, but she was gone at 6 a.m. when I was trying to get my kids up for school," I said with a flicker of excitement.

"I'm going to radio the office to see if they think that is a possibility," the police officer said as he pushed the button on the microphone to reach the dispatcher. "Let me speak to Chief Hope."

I stood next to the unmarked car and heard the conversation.

"Chief, there is a lady here who has a missing daughter. She's a teenager. She disappeared, the girl, I mean, between the hours of 2 a.m. and 6 a.m. I'm sitting here outside the Simmons house waiting for the escaped prisoner to show up. Would that guy have been able to get here between 2 a.m. and 6 a.m.?" asked the police officer.

"Let me look at the file," said the Chief. There was a pause lasting for a few seconds. "Yeah, he could if he had help. Someone would have needed to give him a ride, but maybe he took the ride from someone. I'll check to see if someone has had a car jacked and I'll get back to you."

I stood beside the unmarked police vehicle and waited.

My gut had managed to tie itself into knots, and the pain of distress and worry was gnawing at me.

The radio crackled into life.

"Jones, this is the Chief. There was a carjacking not too far from the prison, so yes, he could have snatched the girl."

My knees got weak and nearly buckled beneath me. I grabbed for the side of the door and held on as Officer Jones talked with the Chief.

Even though I knew the possibility was there, I didn't want anyone else to tell me that what I had been thinking could be the truth.

"Mrs. Harris...."

"Please call me Lindsay. I'm no longer a Mrs.," I said as I tried to make my mind turn away from my fears.

"Tell me more about your daughter. You said her name was Emily? Harris would also be her last name, right?" asked Officer Jones.

I took a deep breath and told him the events from 2 a.m. onward. When I had finished speaking with the officer, I went to get another photo of Emily. I also asked Ellen to walk outside with me so Officer Jones could really see what Emily looked like, since Ellen and Emily were identical twins.

"Officer Jones, look at this young lady. She is Emily's identical twin. This is Ellen," I said as I pushed Ellen forward.

"How was she dressed?" asked Officer Jones.

"I don't really know. Blue jeans and T-shirt, I would guess. She left the house while I was sleeping," I explained.

"I need to go behind your house to see if there is a sign of a struggle. Your daughter would have put up a fight, wouldn't she?" probed Officer Jones.

"Maybe, maybe not. If he had flashed a weapon, she would not have fought. That would have only provoked him. That's what I told her to do if she were ever attacked, so the attacker wouldn't find a reason to hurt her or kill her. I don't think I was wrong about that, do you?" I asked.

"No, ma'am, if more people did that, it might be safer for everyone," answered Officer Jones.

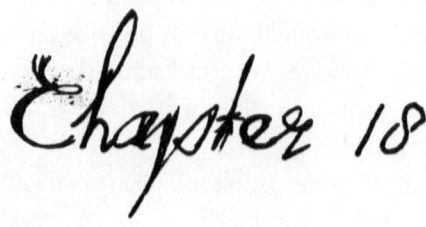

Chapter 18

I led Officer Jones around to the back of my house so he could investigate. Ellen and I went back inside to check on Ryan. As I stepped through the door, Ryan yelled at me.

"You're wanted on the phone, Mom,"

"Who is it?" I asked.

"I think it is Emily," Ryan whispered.

I ran to the phone and eagerly said, "Hello? Emily?"

"Mom, help me, Mom," cried the voice on the phone.

"Where are you, Emily?" I asked as I motioned for my son to get Officer Jones.

"I don't know. He won't tell me. He said not to talk to the police," Emily cried between words.

"Okay, okay, but what does he want from me so you can come home?" I asked softly.

"A car. He said he needs a car," Emily whispered.

"Where? When? I'll bring him my car. I'll make sure the police don't know what I'm doing. Just tell me where to meet you," I pleaded.

I heard silence.

"Emily? Are you there?" I pleaded.

Silence was followed by a loud dial tone blaring in my ear.

"Who was that?" asked Officer Jones as he followed Ryan into the living room.

I paused as I thought about throwing the phone against the wall as hard as I could so I could see it shatter into tiny pieces.

I could not allow myself to break the only connection I had to Emily. I took a deep breath and thought about how I would answer the question Officer Jones had asked.

"Emily," I said softly.

"You found her?" he asked. "Is she okay?"

"I haven't found her and she is not okay," I said as I fought back tears of frustration.

"Was she on the phone with you when I walked into the room?" demanded Officer Jones.

"It was Emily, but she doesn't know where she is being held captive. She was told to deliver the kidnapper's demand for my car. She was also told to tell me not to involve the police," I explained slowly and clearly so I wouldn't have to repeat it over again.

"Did Emily tell you anything else?" Officer Jones asked.

"No, the line went silent and I didn't know the reason for the silence," I answered.

"Can I use your phone?" asked Officer Jones.

"No, she may try to call me again. I can't tie up the house line," I said with apprehension.

"That's fine. I'll go outside and use the car radio," he said.

"No, don't do that. What if he has a scanner?" I said excitedly.

"Okay, Mrs., er, Lindsay, I'll use my personal cell phone," he said in a soothing tone.

"No, no, please don't. I think it would be better if you used my cell phone, don't you?" I said as I reached for my cell phone and thrust it at him.

"I don't think it will matter which cell phone I use, but I'll use yours if you think that would be better," he said calmly.

He glanced at the front of the instrument and immediately started pushing buttons.

"Let me speak to the Chief. This is Jones and it is urgent," he said sternly.

He waited for a few seconds until the chief could be located.

"Chief, it's Jones. We have a situation here at the Harris residence. The missing daughter has contacted her mother at the urging of the kidnapper. No cops," said Officer Jones.

Officer Jones listened intently to what the chief was telling him.

"No, it would be too obvious to station a marked vehicle around here. I don't think he is very far away from here," added Officer Jones.

Again, the conversation ceased as Officer Jones listened to the chief.

I leaned in as close as I could, trying to hear what the chief was saying to Officer Jones. I could make out only a word here and there, and it was absolutely making no sense.

I wanted to grab the phone so I could hear him talking, telling us what we should do to get Emily back from the pervert who had her.

"Yeah, Chief, I'll stay with the family. I think someone needs to be here when they get another call. They WILL get another call and soon. I'm sure of that."

Officer Jones pushed the button and disconnected the line.

"What did the chief want to do about this?" I asked.

"He's putting out an Amber Alert for Emily and All Points Bulletin for the escaped convict. I will stay here and wait for the call with you and then we will go from there," said Officer Jones.

"That's all?" I asked incredulously.

"The Amber Alert will get everyone involved statewide. That's about all that can be done for now," said Officer Jones.

"He will know I called the police," I screamed.

"Mrs. Harris, Lindsay, you could have called the police before you received Emily's call," explained Officer Jones.

"I don't care. You need to stop that from showing up on the television or radio. I don't want it anywhere a scanner could be listening in. Please, this nut might kill my Emily," I pleaded.

"I'll call the chief again, but it may be too late to stop the broadcast. They really move fast when a child is involved," said Officer Jones.

"Please try," I begged.

Officer Jones grabbed the cell phone, again, and started pushing numbers rapidly.

"I need the chief," he said to the person who answered the call.

There was a long pause.

"Chief, the mother wants the Amber Alert stopped now," he said loudly.

I could hear a loud voice at the other end of the conversation, but I couldn't make out the words. The anger was evident.

Officer Jones disconnected the call and said, "He will try to cancel the Amber Alert, but it may have gone out over the air already."

"God help me, I hope not," I said as I returned to the sofa to sit and wait for my house telephone to ring.

My cell phone started ringing. At first, I couldn't figure out where the ringing was coming from.

"It's my cell phone," I said as I went in search of the sound. Officer Jones had been the last one to use it and I didn't know where he had laid it down.

I found the cell phone on the end table, covered with a piece of paper.

"Hello," I said hesitantly.

"Lindsay?" said a weak, trembling voice.

"Yes?"

"This is Jed."

"Jed, are you still in the hospital?" I asked when I realized to whom I was speaking.

"Yes. Are you coming to see me?" he whispered.

"I will as soon as I find out what's happening with Emily," I answered.

"They want to cut my leg off," he said in broken tones.

"What?" I screamed.

"They want to cut my leg off," he said as he faded into tears.

"Why?" I asked.

"Too infected. Spreading through my body," he said.

"Tell them to send you to Bristol to a hospital where the doctors will help you, not cripple you," I said excitedly.

"You think that would be better?" he asked.

"Yes, Jed, they will probably have a better answer for you than amputation. You need to go to Bristol. Tell them that, please," I begged.

"I'll try," he whispered.

"Who is your doctor? I'll give him a call and ask him to tell the Stillwell people to transfer you to Bristol," I said.

"Terry Marlowe, but I can't remember his number," he whispered labored breathing.

"I'll get it. Just hang in there and don't let them cut off your leg," I said excitedly.

"Okay," he answered as his voice faded away to silence.

"Oh, my God, now what?" I said as I threw my hands into the air.

I ran to my computer to locate the phone number for Dr. Terry Marlowe. I entered Dr. Terry Marlowe into the Google search engine and a number of different websites popped up on my screen.

I re-entered Dr. Terry Marlowe and Virginia to narrow the search. Still, too many websites appeared and not one of them looked like it was the website I needed.

Dr. Terry Marlowe and Tennessee was my next entry. Because Bristol bordered Virginia and Tennessee, there was a fifty-fifty chance that I would find him.

Tennessee was it. Dr. Terry Marlowe was listed and he had an emergency number listed. I punched in his number and a real, live person answered it, not the machine that I had been expecting to reel off a pre-recorded statement.

"Hi, my name is Lindsay Harris and I am calling for a friend, Jed Thompson, who is a patient of Dr. Marlowe's," I explained in a flurry of words.

"How can I help you, Mrs. Harris?"

"Jed is in Stillwell Community Hospital with a staph infection. They told him they were going to have to amputate his leg. Please call that hospital and request that they transfer him to Bristol under Dr. Marlowe's care," I explained.

"Do you have the phone number handy?" asked the professional female voice.

I rattled off the phone number and gushed out many words of thanks.

"Please help him. He needs to keep his leg," I said before I disconnected the line.

I heaved an enormous sigh of relief and fought the tears that were threatening to spill over my eyelids.

Chapter 19

I was sitting and waiting. I was not very good at either of those, but I was especially bad at waiting.

Waiting for a phone call. Waiting for the police to tell me they had found my Emily. Waiting for the kidnapper to tell me where to take my car so I could have my Emily back home safe and sound. Waiting ... waiting ... waiting. Waiting makes me crazy.

My house phone started ringing and that brought me back to reality.

"Hello? Emily?" I said anxiously.

Officer Jones was standing next to me, leaning against me as I held the phone to my ear. He was there to listen and pass on the information to the police department.

The legal authorities had not set up any recording devices inside my house because they were afraid they, the officers, would be spotted by the kidnapper. They said they were relying solely on Officer Jones, as was I.

"Mrs. Harris, Lindsay Harris," said the disguised voice. It sounded like the speaker was talking through a towel, which muffled his words.

"Yes, yes, this is Lindsay. I want to speak with Emily. Please put Emily on the phone," I said in an effort to keep him on the phone. I knew the legal authorities were tracing every call made to my number even though they had told me that only Officer Jones would be listening in to everything that was said.

"You need to listen to me if you want your daughter back. Make no mistake, I will kill her if you don't do exactly as I say," the disguised voice whispered harshly.

"I will. I promise I will do everything you tell me to do. Please let Emily come back to me. Please don't hurt her. For God's sake, please don't kill my baby girl," I cried.

"Drive your car to the City Park in Bluefield and park it directly in the center of the parking lot. There will be lots of cars in that lot, so I will be watching you as you look for a parking space. Keep looking until you can find a spot in the center. There will be an 'X' marking the parking space. Keep driving around until you can park in that space. Come alone or she dies."

Silence.

The line was dead again.

I looked at Officer Jones to see what he had to say.

He said nothing.

"I'm going to do exactly as he instructed," I said sternly.

"You can't do that, Mrs. Harris. It's too dangerous," said Officer Jones.

"She is my daughter. I have to do whatever it takes to get her back. I will do what he told me to do no matter what you tell me," I said with conviction.

"Yes, ma'am, I know you will. But... you can't do it alone," said Officer Jones.

"I have to do it alone. I think he is watching my house. You think that, too, or you would have been relieved before now. Another officer would have been here to take your place so you

61

could take a break. There is no way you can get into the car without him seeing you," I said angrily.

"You're not going alone," Officer Jones said forcefully.

That's what you think, I thought as I walked into the kitchen.

I knew I had to sneak out of the house without Officer Jones seeing me.

Ryan was sitting at the kitchen table playing cards with Ellen. I sat down so I could ask them to help me sneak out of the house.

"Mom, what was the phone call about?" asked Ellen.

"The man who has your sister told me where I had to go and what I had to do, but I need your help. Do you want to help me?" I asked my totally interested children.

"Yes, yes, Mom, what can we do?" said an excited Ryan.

I held my finger up in front of my lips and said, "Sh-sh-sh, I don't want Officer Jones to hear us." The tones became hushed, conspiratorial whispers.

"Ellen, I need to sneak out. Can you and Ryan cause a disturbance in the living room to keep Officer Jones occupied?" I asked.

"Yeah, sure. Ryan and I can get into a loud argument like we have done many times."

"I've had to break up many disagreements. Do it just like you have in the past, except, this time, you need to be louder, really loud. Okay?" I asked.

"When?" asked Ryan.

"Now. You guys get started and get louder and louder. I will sneak out the back door to the car to get Emily," I said as I grabbed my handbag, that I had moved to the kitchen counter.

Ryan took off running to the living room with Ellen chasing him.

"You're a liar," yelled Ryan.

"I am not," returned Ellen.

"You are a liar. I know you are," shouted Ryan as he ran from her, staying just out of her grasp.

"I didn't say that?" screamed Ellen.

"Yes, you did. I heard you!" shouted Ryan as he ducked and weaved.

Even outside, I could hear them both very clearly as I started my car and took off down the driveway as quietly as I could so Officer Jones might not notice. Hopefully the screams from my kids would keep him entertained and he would not in tune to the outside world.

As soon as I reached the street, I turned left, away from my front window, and sped off like a bat out of hell toward Bluefield, which was twenty miles from my home.

My cell phone started to ring. I struggled as I tried to find it in my handbag while I continued to drive.

"Hello," I shouted into the annoying instrument.

"Lindsay, this is Annie. Are you okay?" she asked.

"No, I'm not. I'm on my way to get my missing daughter. I'm glad you called, Annie. Can you meet me at Bluefield City Park in about an hour and bring a cop with you in your car?" I asked hurriedly.

"Sure, why there? Why a cop?" asked Annie.

"I need someone to pick me up. I have to leave my car there and I will need a ride home," I explained.

"Okay, see you in an hour," said Annie as she disconnected the call.

I worked the gas pedal, pushing it down as far as I could without attracting a policeman.

I turned off of 460 and onto the street that would take me to the city park. He had been telling the truth. The parking lot was full of cars. I weaved through the lanes, trying to determine where the center of the lot would be.

I saw it. The "X" was worn off a bit, but it was still visible.

There was a car in that space. I drove through the parking lanes over and over again, waiting for the owner of the parked car to remove his vehicle so I could pull into that same space.

I was watching the time and I was watching the parked car as I was growing more and more anxious.

Please, please, move your car, I prayed.

I looked out across the parking lot and saw Annie's car. She had pulled into a parking slot and watched me navigate through the lot. She made no sign of recognition and I was grateful for that.

There was a man sitting on the front seat next to Annie. I didn't get a very good look at her passenger, so I wasn't sure it was a cop.

I caught a glimpse of a person walking toward the parked car. I was about two parking lanes away from the place I needed to be, so I tried to hurry. That wasn't going to happen—hurrying, I mean. It seemed that the parking was suddenly filling up with people walking to their cars. Whatever had attracted so many people must have dismissed the audience, disgorging the crowd into the parking lot.

I crawled my way to the end of the parking lane so I could turn into the lane where I needed to be and could pull directly into the marked parking space. I continued to force my vehicle to crawl through the crowd without killing a pedestrian. When I arrived at the spot, the car was still there and no one was near it.

"Please, please, move that car!" I screamed to no one in particular. I was so stressed out that I had to scream.

I pulled my car up and threw the gear into "park." I was going to stay in that spot, blocking the driver of the parked car in the space so that person couldn't leave without running into my vehicle.

I leaned my head forward and closed my eyes only for a moment so I could regain control of my nerves.

Someone was knocking on my window. I jumped so much from the noise that I hit my head on the steering wheel. When I looked toward the window, I saw a man motioning for me to move my car so he could get his car out of the parking space that I was blocking.

I smiled at the man, started my car, and backed up a bit so I could pull into the same spot he was vacating.

I looked out across the parking lot, and mingling in the crowd was Emily, who was walking toward me with a man whose head was covered with a big hat. He had a beard, a full beard, covering his face.

I climbed out of my car and waited for them to reach me. When they were close enough, I held out my car keys and grabbed hold of Emily. We turned and I told her to run.

"Run, Em, run as fast as you can. I'll be right behind you," I whispered.

I did not want him to lay his hands on either one of us, so we ran. I guided her towards Annie's car, where I knew we would find the help we needed.

Suddenly the parking lot was full of uniformed officers wearing safety vests branded with SPD (Stillwell Police Department) and flashing loaded handguns.

The appearance of all of the cops was as much a surprise to me as I was sure it was to the escaped prisoner. No shots were fired and he was escorted to a police vehicle under heavy guard, much to the relief of Emily and myself.

Annie and I stood next to Emily as she told the detective how she had been kidnapped.

"How did Underwood grab you?" asked Detective Sims, who had been in Annie's car.

"I was on my way out of the back door to go meet my friend, Maddie, so we could go to school together. She is new student and I thought she could use a friend," said Emily.

"Okay, you walked out your door. What happened next?" asked Detective Sims.

"I turned to check the door to see that I had it locked, and he grabbed me. He put his arm around me over my throat and I had to go with him because he was pressing on my neck and I couldn't breathe," Emily said as she rubbed her throat.

"Where did he take you?" asked the detective.

"To and old shed behind the neighbor's house. I had never seen anyone go into that shed, so I had thought it was for storage of tools and lawn mowers, and stuff like that. Since the yard was fenced, I just never checked it out. I guess I should have. Anyway, we stayed in that little shed all day. We went inside the shed through a loose panel in the back. The front always stayed padlocked so no one would know we were in there. I was scared to leave. I wanted to go home. I was so afraid," Emily said as she burst into tears.

"When did he take you out of the shed?" asked Detective Sims.

I watched Emily as she tried to stop the flow of tears. I knew she wanted to tell the story, but it was so hard.

"Are you up to continuing?" asked the detective.

"Yes, I'll try," Emily said as she wiped her face with the tissues I handed to her. "When it got dark he tied my hands behind my back and pushed me through the panel. He said he had to make a phone call. We walked to a convenience store that had an pay phone outside. That's where he made me call. I had to tell him the number and he held the phone next to my ear. He told me what to say and then we walked to a deserted house where we stayed until he decided to go to the parking lot to get Mom's car. We went back to that convenience store, where he asked a customer to give us a ride to Bluefield. I was so afraid. I thought he would kill me because I knew what he looked like, but he didn't. All he wanted was a car," Emily said almost sympathetically.

"Don't feel sorry for him, Emily," said Detective Sims. "He killed his best friend for flirting with his girlfriend. He doesn't deserve your sympathy."

"He really could have killed me, Mom. I didn't know he had already killed someone before he took me," said Emily as she started sobbing again.

"Detective Sims, I need to take Emily home now. I need to check on my two other children. May we leave?" I asked.

"Yes, ma'am. If I have any more questions, I know where to find you," Detective Sims said as he smiled and winked at Emily.

"Come on, babe," I said to Emily. "Let's go home."

Chapter 20

Ellen and Ryan were sitting on the living room sofa being entertained by Officer Jones who, out of the kindness in his heart, had stayed with them while I had been delivering my car to the escaped killer.

"Thanks, Officer Jones. I'm so glad you stayed with Ryan and Ellen. Ellen is old enough to babysit Ryan, but I'm glad you were here."

"No problem. I just wanted to be with them until you returned with your lost one," he said as he stood to leave.

I walked him to the door thanking him again and again.

After Emily told the story to Ryan and Ellen, I ordered a pizza for us to eat. We were all starving and tired, but still too wound up to sleep.

"Mom, Jed isn't here. Is he okay?" asked Emily.

"Oh, my gosh," I said as I realized I hadn't checked on him. "I need to call the hospital to see if they transferred him to Bristol."

"Why was he going to Bristol?" asked Ellen.

"He has a really bad infection in his leg. I thought he should go to Bristol where there are specialists who can help him," I said as I tried to explain it to them without getting them upset. They had grown to like Jed a lot, maybe too much.

"They couldn't take care of him here?" asked Ryan.

"No, not the way he needed. He would be much better off in Bristol," I said.

"Can we go see him?" asked Ellen.

"Sure, but I need to find out where he is first," I said as I reached for the house phone.

I entered the Stillwell Community Hospital number and waited for the pre-recorded directions telling me the number that would take me to Jed's room. The phone rang several times until the operator broke into the line.

"That number isn't answering. Who are you trying to reach?" she asked in a severely professional tone.

"Jed Thompson," I said.

"Are you a family member?" she asked.

"Yes, but there was a family crisis and I needed to find out if he was transferred to Bristol," I said as I crossed my fingers behind my back.

"Yes, ma'am, he was transferred earlier today," she answered.

"Good, thank you. Have a great day," I said as I disconnected the line.

"Can we call him in Bristol?" asked Ryan. "I want to tell him I'm not mad at him because he couldn't take me fishing."

I reached for my son and hugged him close.

"I'll try to call right now, but I need to find the phone number for the hospital. Ellen, can you look it up on the computer? I don't have a Bristol phonebook."

"Okay," she said as she ran to where the desktop was stationed. A few moments later she said, "Here it is, Mom."

She read the number to me and I entered it on the keypad of the house phone.

The recorded message directed me to an operator since I didn't know my party's phone number.

"Jed Thompson," I said when a live person answered.

"That is room 415 and the direct line to the room is 423-555-0415," said the operator as she connected me to Jed's room line.

It rang and rang. I wasn't going to hang up until I got an answer, so I let it continue to ring.

"Hello," said a groggy voice.

"Jed? Jed Thompson?" I asked worriedly.

"Yeah?"

"This is Lindsay. What's going on?" I asked.

"Moved me to Bristol. Not going to cut off my leg. Surgery tomorrow to clean it up inside. Got to sleep," he said in rapid bursts of fragmented sentences.

"What time tomorrow?" I asked.

"8 a.m. I've got to sleep. Doesn't hurt when I sleep," he slurred.

"Bye, Jed. I'll be there tomorrow," I said as I hung up the phone.

"Well?' asked Ellen.

"They are operating on Jed's leg tomorrow morning. He is too drugged up to talk right now. Do you want to go with me to the hospital and see him before he goes into surgery?" I asked my children.

"Yes, let's go," said Ellen and Emily almost in unison.

"Sure," said Ryan, who was eager to talk with Jed and forgive him.

The night seemed terribly short when my alarm clock rang at 5 a.m. Saturday morning. I roused my sleepy kids out of their beds, told them to get dressed, and that they could go back to sleep in the car. We had about a two-hour drive ahead of us.

We all walked out the door clad in blue jeans, tee shirts, and jackets. The only person who was wide-awake was me because I had to drive.

I turned the volume on the radio down, playing the music softly so they would not be bothered by too much outside noise as I drove. My mind was racing as I tried to figure out why Emily had been taken and why Jed had been involved in a car accident that had very nearly, and might still, cost him his leg.

Jed had been investigating the disappearance of Dennis Martin's parents. Had his accident been directly related to that disappearance? My gut told me it was. But, why?

My cell phone started ringing, so I grabbed it as fast as I could to allow my children some more sleep time.

"Hello," I said softly.

"Lindsay, where are you?" asked Annie.

"On my way to Bristol. Jed's having surgery on his leg this morning," I said in answer.

"What happened?" asked Annie.

"It got infected really, really badly. I didn't want him to be alone, so the kids and I piled into the car to be with him," I explained.

"Do you have a minute to talk?" asked Annie.

"Yes, sure, but I need to keep driving," I said as I glanced at Ryan, who was buckled up in the front seat next to me. His sisters had happily crawled into the backseat to sleep more comfortably.

"Dennis Martin, my neighbor, is not the creep I thought he was," Annie said.

"Why did you change your mind?" I asked.

"Well, he has had to come in for another appointment with Everett and I got a chance to talk with him. He seems to be really shy, but also very scared. I'm not sure why he is so scared, but you can tell by his actions. He is nervous and constantly glances behind him, looking for something or someone. Even when he is here he looks over his shoulder like we would let somebody in to get at him," Annie explained.

"What about your dog? Do you still think he killed Harvey?" I asked.

"I'm not sure, but my brain is leaning towards no." Annie answered.

"Has he mentioned your dog?" I asked.

"Yes, he asked me what happened to Harvey."

"What did you tell him?" I asked.

"The truth: I think someone killed him;" said Annie solemnly. "Then he asked me who I thought would so that?"

"What did you say?" I asked.

"The truth again, which is I don't know," Annie said.

"What's going on with his missing parents?" I asked.

"Everett has asked the police to track their credit card activity and their back account," Annie said.

"Well, what did the police say?" I asked.

"Nothing much except that they haven't spent any money for weeks. That doesn't sound good, does it?" asked Annie.

"No, it doesn't. Jed was in a car wreck after he asked some questions about Dennis Martin's parents. I think his accident is related to Dennis Martin some way. I don't know how yet, but I'll find out. I don't think Emily's kidnapping is related. That was just the luck of the draw in life, I think, but I don't know for sure. Could be the escaped prisoner is involved some way, but that seems too far-fetched for me. What do you think?" I asked Annie.

"I don't know. Are you going to be able to come to work on Monday?" asked Annie.

"I hope so," I answered.

"Me, too. Wayne's getting grouchier with each passing hour because you're not here," Annie explained.

"He'll just have to get over it. I'll try to be there," I said with a laugh. It was a fake laugh because I was afraid that my absence would cause Wayne to replace me with anyone who walked in off the street. That's how he felt. I could be replaced by anyone.

"Are you going to tell Everett about what happened to Jed?" Annie asked.

"I'm not sure. Maybe," I said.

We ended out conversation and I continued my drive to Bristol, my mind rambling on and on as I drove. Eventually I saw the exit that led me to the Bristol Hospital.

"Kids, we're almost there," I said loudly.

They started rousing themselves.

"I need to go to the bathroom," said Ellen.

"We're here. Let's go inside and find a bathroom," I said to Ellen.

Chapter 21

We trooped into our respective restrooms and then found an elevator that would take us to the fourth floor.

I found room 415 and told my kids to stand and wait quietly in the hall while I stuck my head inside the room to see if he was decent.

He wasn't there.

The room was clean and made up, awaiting a new patient or, hopefully, a returning one.

"He's not in here," I told my children. "Let's go to the nurses' station and see if they took him to surgery early."

"Jed Thompson is not in his room. Did he go to surgery early?" I asked.

"Yes, ma'am. He should be getting back to his room soon. Would you like to wait for him in the lounge?" asked the nurse who had been sitting at a desk behind the counter. "I will let you know when he returns to his room. The lounge is down the hall to your left."

"Thank you for being so kind," I said as I herded my kids further down the hall.

Ellen and Emily were busy talking about everything that Emily had gone through during her disappearance while Ryan was busy playing a game on my smart phone.

I sat quietly, just waiting.

An hour passed, then another one. I was getting worried. I was surprised that none of the kids were giving me a hard time about just having to sit and wait. I was about to get up and walk to Jed's room to see if he had returned when the nurse walked through the door.

The nurse walked toward me and said, "Are you Lindsay?"

I nodded my head in answer.

"Mr. Thompson is asking for you," she said as she turned to leave.

"You guys stay put while I check to see if we can all go see him," I said as I left the lounge.

I walked into Jed's room and abruptly stopped to take in what was before me.

Jed was in the center on the bed with his eyes half open. His leg was propped up on a pillow. There were strange-looking metal things sticking out of the cast. They looked like they had been crisscrossed under the white, gauzy-looking but hard cast. It looked as if they had been pushed through the flesh and skin of his leg.

"What did they do to your leg?" I asked with concern.

Jed's eyes opened wider when he spotted me at the foot of his bed.

"They said they had to break the bone again, scrape out the infection, and reset it with metal pins. I don't feel anything right now, but I will when the pain medication wears off," he said, slurring his words.

"How long are you going to have to stay in the hospital?" I asked.

"I might get out this afternoon if I've got someone to help me," he said as he looked at me with pleading eyes.

75

"I'll help you, but you will have to go home with me and the kids. They are here and want to see you. Can they come in for a minute?" I asked.

"Yeah, I'd like to see them," Jed said with a little less of a slur.

I walked to the lounge and told them to walk down the hall quietly. We were all positioned around his bed when the doctor entered the room.

"Is this your family, Mr. Thompson?" asked the doctor.

"Yes, this is Lindsay, Ellen, Emily, and Ryan," said Jed as he displayed a big, broad smile.

"Since you've got such a good-looking family, I'll let you go home so they can take care of you. All I need for you to do is show me that you can walk with those crutches," said the doctor as he pointed toward the corner of the room.

Jed scooted to the side of the bed, hauled his casted leg down to the floor with both hands, situated the crutches under each arm, and then took off walking. He obviously wanted out of the hospital.

"That's good, Mr. Thompson. You can get dressed and I'll get the paperwork going. You will need to cut you pant leg to get your pants on. I brought a pair of scissors for you to do just that. Just cut them up the inside seam and perhaps they can be repaired later," said the doctor as he left the room.

"Lindsay, can you cut the pant leg for me?" Jed asked.

I grabbed the scissors and reached for his pants.

"You won't be able to repair these, Jed. I'll have to cut them to just below the crotch. Your cast is pretty big. Maybe you can use them as shorts next summer," I said as I spread the jeans out on the floor where I had some room to cut straight.

"Just cut them. I want out of here. Can you stop at my house to let me get some clothes? I think sweats would be better until I can get back into my jeans," said Jed.

Getting the pants on him took the longest amount of time. Thankfully, he already had his underwear in place, so that was an embarrassment he could avoid with the girls in the room.

The nurse brought in the discharge papers for him to sign and we were on our way to his house to pick up some clothes.

We all trooped into his one one-bedroom apartment. He pointed to the areas where his clothes were located and we stuffed them into a couple of plastic bags. I gathered his mail for him as he checked his messages on his house phone and off we went. I wanted to get him to the house, and out of the confining car, before the pain medication completely wore off and he started feeling the effects of everything they had done to him.

He looked at his mail as he sat next to me on the front seat. We had pushed the seat back as far as it would go to allow him some extra room and had placed Ryan behind him because he had short legs. The girls had to sit close together, but they didn't complain too much.

"Lindsay, you need to see this," Jed said as he held a piece of paper up.

"What is it?" I asked as I continued to drive.

"I think it's a threat," Jed said.

I pulled my car over to the side of the road so I could take a look at the paper Jed was clutching nervously.

The note said:

NO MORE QUESTIONS
OR I WILL
FINISH THE JOB.

The words had been cut out of a newspaper and glued onto the white sheet of paper.

"I guess you were right about someone running you off the road on purpose," I said as I read the note again. "How did they know where you lived?"

"I'm a newspaper reporter. My information is all over the Internet," he said matter-of-factly.

"We need to take this note to Everett. He is the lawyer working on the Martin case. Whether you like it or not, you are directly involved in their disappearance. We need to get home just in case we are being watched or followed," I said as I glanced around to see if any vehicles had stopped behind me. It looked clear, so I pulled my car out into the traffic to continue my drive home.

I kept a watchful eye on my rearview mirror. I was getting so very paranoid. I didn't want anything to happen while I had my kids in the car.

"Jed, what kind of questions did you ask?" I said to break up the tension and silence.

"Stuff like, 'How long they had been gone?' 'Who was the last person to see them other than their son?'" he answered.

"Those questions shouldn't cause all of these problems. They have been asked several times already. Those are just normal missing person questions," I said. "What else did you ask?"

"I wanted to know what Mr. Martin did for a living and the same for Mrs. Martin. I wanted to know where they worked, and that was the question most everybody couldn't answer. Everybody told me that the Martins were self-employed, but they couldn't tell me what they did exactly. Some thought they were in sales, but they didn't know what they sold. Some others thought they ran a consulting business. When I asked who or why they consulted, they couldn't answer me."

"Sounds strange, doesn't it?" I asked.

"Yeah, it does. Makes me think they might be into something illegal," Jed said as he winced.

"Pain coming back?" I asked.

He nodded his head as he winced again.

"It's not much further," I said in sympathy. "Did you ask any other probing questions?"

"Well, yes. I wanted to know if they were dealing drugs," Jed said.

"What was the answer to that question?" I asked.

"Most everyone thought Dennis, their son, was dealing," he said with a sigh.

"I guess that was the wrong question," I said as I turned onto my driveway. "We're home."

We all helped get Jed into the house and into my bedroom where he could stretch out the cast-covered leg to help relieve the pain.

I went into the kitchen to find some food to prepare for us to eat. Hot dogs and hamburgers were going to be on the menu, so I started the preparation. I knew we were all hungry and would need to eat more than one each.

While the meats were cooking, I called Annie.

"I've got Jed here again, Annie. He needed someone to help him, so we got nominated," I said with a laugh.

"Is he okay?" asked Annie.

"Sore, very sore, and he has a big cast with metal pins sticking out of it on his leg. It looks like the pins are crisscrossed through the flesh of his leg. It's got to hurt," I said.

"How long is he going to be there?" Annie asked.

"I don't know. I need to ask you something, Annie," I said in a whisper.

"What's that?"

"Do you think Dennis Martin is into drugs? You thought he might be at one time. Do you still think that?" I asked.

"No, I don't," Annie said.

"What about his parents?" I asked.

"What about them?" Annie snapped.

"Were they into drugs?" I asked.

"No, never. They are really nice people, or they were the few times I saw them."

"If not drugs, what would they be involved with?" I asked, not really expecting an answer.

"I got some more news about the credit card and bank account background check," said Annie.

"Well, tell me," I said.

"It only goes back about ten years and then there is nothing else about them," said Annie.

"That's strange," I said as my mind started rolling through the possibilities. "Witness protection?" I said when my spinning mind stopped.

"That's what Everett thinks. He hasn't asked Dennis yet, but that's what he thinks might be the problem," said Annie.

"You aren't getting too close to Dennis, are you?" I asked, knowing she would deny any strong feelings.

"No, no. He's just a neighbor," she said, but her tone wasn't too convincing.

"We need to find out the truth, Annie. Those people who have Martin's parents are after Jed and they mean to kill him," I said sternly.

"You can't be sure of that," said Annie.

"Yes, I can. He was asking questions about them. I'm sure it's related somehow."

"What can we do?" asked Annie.

"I'm going to give Everett a call. I don't think this can wait until Monday," I said.

"Call me back if you find out anything," said Annie.

"Okay," I said as I disconnected the line.

Chapter 22

"Come and get it," I shouted from the kitchen. My kids came running and started filling their plates with a hot dog each, a hamburger each, and a pile of chips.

I prepared plates for Jed and myself and carried them to my bedroom so Jed wouldn't have to eat alone.

"What do you think about witness protection?" I asked.

"Witness protection? I never even thought of that. Could be," he said as he pondered the possibility.

"That's what Annie and I were thinking. Maybe his parents saw something they shouldn't have seen. Now the people they saw are trying to eliminate them for whatever reason," I explained. "I'm going to call Everett and see what he thinks after I get finished with the dishes."

"You've got a phone in here. Do it now so I can hear your end of the conversation," said Jed.

I found my address book, looked up Everett's phone number, and punched it onto the phone keypad.

"Everett, this is Lindsay," I said after his pleasant hello.

"What can I do for you?" Everett asked.

"I have a question about the Martin case," I said.

"What question?" he asked with interest.

"Could they be in witness protection?"

I heard an intake of air then a sigh.

"Yes, I think so. I haven't found out for sure. Not yet. Why do you ask?" Everett probed.

"My friend, Jed, has become an unwilling participant in this case. He was asking questions about the missing Martins and someone tried to kill him," I explained.

"Are you sure?" asked Everett.

"Yes, he is sitting right here. I'll put him on the phone to talk with you," I said as I handed the phone to Jed.

I picked up the empty dinner plates and walked to the kitchen for cleanup duties while Jed talked with Everett.

Emily walked into the kitchen to help me. She wanted to talk to me alone, so I didn't ask Ellen and Ryan to give me a hand with the dishes.

"Mom, I'm so sorry about sneaking out the back door and getting into trouble," she said solemnly.

"Em, it was not you fault. You did leave a note to let me know where you were going," I told my worried daughter.

"Maddie is such a nice girl and she is new, so no one would pal around with her," said Emily.

"Where does Maddie live? When I went to look for her, the house at the address she gave to the school officials was empty," I said as I tried to figure out the puzzle that was Maddie Stevens.

"She's homeless. She has been staying in the empty house at that address," answered Emily.

"It's really nice of you to want to help and befriend Maddie," I said as I tried to let her know I wasn't angry with her.

Emily smiled a little as her shoulders sagged a little less.

"Emily, why don't you want to hang around with Ellen anymore? What happened?" I asked as I tried to find out what had caused the split.

"I want to be my own person. I am tired of being the other half of a person because I am an identical twin," Emily explained with feeling gleaming in her eyes.

"I don't see you as half of anything or anybody, Em," I said.

"It's not you, Mom. It's our classmates, our teachers, and everyone else who knows that I am part of a set," Emily continued.

"Okay. What can I do to help?" I asked.

"Please don't make me go to the drama club just because Ellen wants to be in it. I don't like drama club. I don't want to sing, dance, and perform the writings of other people. I want to do the writing. I want to build the sets. I want to be part of the engine in the background that makes it all come together," Emily explained. "When we go shopping for school clothes, don't buy two of every-thing. I don't want to be preppy like Ellen. I want to wear blue jeans and tee shirts like you do, Mom," Emily said earnestly.

I had to smile at that last statement.

"You are Emily Harris, my daughter, and that is how I will refer to you in the future. I will no longer say that you are Ellen's twin sister. Will that help?" I asked.

I guess I finally said the right mom thing, because I was hugged fiercely by my rapidly aging daughter, Emily.

Emily and I finished the dishes and I returned to my bedroom to see what advice Everett had given Jed.

Chapter 23

"What did Everett tell you?" I asked Jed as soon as I walked over the threshold of the bedroom.

"He's checking into the witness protection theory. He said he was almost sure that is the reason Dennis Martin's parents are missing," said Jed.

"Did he ask Dennis Martin if his family was in witness protection?" I asked skeptically.

"Yes, but Martin denied it. Wouldn't they take him from the home he is living in and move him to another undisclosed location?" asked Jed.

"That's what I had heard about people under witness protection. Of course, they could have dropped out of the program but kept their identities," I said as I recalled some of the television programs I had watched.

"Yes, that could be what happened. Everett said Dennis Martin would not talk about anything that happened when he was a child. Depending on how many years have passed and the circumstances, Dennis Martin might not know anything at all. Maybe that's why he is still there. Maybe whoever took his parents is trying to find out if he knows anything," Jed suggested.

"What else did Everett say?" I asked.

"Everett said Dennis Martin has received threats but no ransom notes. They probably know he has no money," Jed answered.

"What kind of threats?" I asked.

"Like the one I received in the mail with the threat of no talking to anyone or else. He hasn't called the cops because of the threat, but he thought that hiring a lawyer to help him keep his house might not get them too riled up," said Jed.

"What did he tell you to do?" I asked.

"Stay out of sight was his only suggestion. I received the threat in Bristol, so that is where I should have contacted the police. Whoever it is that is threatening Dennis Martin is probably here in this town. Stillwell is not very big, so Everett is hoping the truth can be uncovered here. If I call the cops here in Stillwell, he thinks it might get out and we would all be in trouble. That means Ellen, Emily, Ryan, you, and me," Jed explained.

"What am I supposed to do about that?" I asked.

"You should go on about your business, you and the kids. I should stay away from windows and out of sight. I'm so sorry this is happening, Lindsay. You know I wouldn't want harm to come to any of you."

"I know, I know. But what if someone saw you when we helped you into the house?" I asked.

"We just have to hope that they didn't. Everett said he is going to ask the town police to patrol this area more frequently. He says there are drug dealers in the area, so they will look a little more often. They night actually catch a dealer or two, you know."

"I would love to take my kids somewhere to stay, but they have to go to school. I don't know a soul who would want to take in three extra mouths to feed. Justin, my ex-husband, has moved out of town because of a new job, so I can't let him take them. Besides, if I did that, he would probably never bring them back. Jed, I can't lose my babies."

"They should be fine staying right here because those crazy people are after me, not any of you," said Jed.

"Hopefully we won't be in the way if and when they find you," I mumbled as I sat on the edge of the bed.

"Don't worry, Linds, I won't let anything happen to your babies," said Jed as he reached to give me a hug. I could feel him wincing from the strain of the hug.

"Did you bring anything to sleep in?" I asked as I stood up.

"Tee shirts and sweats," he answered.

"You need to get yourself ready for bed, so change your clothes. If you need help, give me a holler. I'm going to chase the brood to bed so I can have the sofa again," I said as I left the bedroom.

My children were as tired as I was, so chasing them to bed was not difficult. Jed didn't holler, so I guessed he changed without too much trouble.

I laid my head on a pillow and was asleep in no time.

Chapter 24

What Is that? I asked myself as I laid there, not moving a muscle.

It was a scratching. It didn't sound like an animal scratching at a door. It was erratic, as if someone were using a tool of some kind to pry open a window or a door.

I jumped up from the sofa and ran to my bedroom door where I awoke Jed.

"Jed, there is someone trying to get into the house," I whispered.

"What can I use as a weapon?" Jed whispered harshly.

"I'll try to find something, but I need to wake the kids first. Maybe I can get them out the back door and to the neighbor's house," I said as I hurried out the door.

I paused for a moment to listen.

Is he in the house? I asked myself as I strained to amplify my hearing ability. *There is it. He is still scratching at the window.*

I stepped forward slowly as I crossed the hall to get to Ellen and Emily. I opened Ellen's bedroom door making sure to close it quietly so no sounds could be heard.

I moved next to Ellen's bed and bent to whisper into her ear.

"Ellen, get up and get out of here," I said sternly as I could in a whisper.

"What, hunh?" said a sleepy Ellen.

"Get up and go stand over there," I said as I pointed to the bedroom door.

"What's going on?" Ellen asked a little louder, which caused Emily to stir in the next bedroom. Emily had left her bathroom door open so she could hear her sister.

"Both of you," I said in a tone just above a whisper, "get up and go stand over there. Wait for me. I'm going to go wake up your brother."

I opened the door partially to look and listen. Nothing, no noises of any kind could be heard. I stepped out and listened again. I thought I heard a rustling sound.

My God, is he in the house? I asked myself as I looked up to the ceiling and beyond asking for help.

I had to get Ryan up, and he would be the noisiest one to rouse up out of bed.

I opened his door and saw, to my surprise, that he had his eyes open and was staring at me. He was not moving a muscle. His blanket was pulled up under his chin. I looked at his eyes again. They were not just staring; they were wide open from fear.

I froze at the doorway. I didn't know whether to step forward to protect Ryan or step backward and try to get the girls out of the house safely. The decision was made for me.

"Get in here and close the door," growled a man dressed entirely in black, including a ski mask covering his head, and was holding the biggest gun I had ever seen.

'Don't hurt my son," I screamed. I wanted the other three people in the house to know we were not alone.

"Shut up, Lady!" he growled. "Or I will shoot you both. Now, get over here where I can keep an eye on you."

I did as he said. I moved slowly toward the head of Ryan's bed where I could place my hand on his shoulder to comfort him, if that was at all possible.

"What do you want? If it is money, I will give you all that I have," I said in a broken, fear-filled voice.

"Your friend is what I want. Where is your friend?" he asked.

"What friend?" I snapped.

"The one who is causing all of the trouble," he said impatiently.

"Who are you talking about?" I asked.

"You know who. He was here with you. I saw you help him in and I haven't seen him leave. Where is he?" he growled as he waved the gun around, making sure that I could see it.

"You mean Jed. He left late last night. A friend came to pick him up and took him back to his house," I lied, praying that I was convincing.

"Is that true?" he asked Ryan.

Ryan looked at me and nodded his head. He was so scared he was shaking noticeably under the covers.

"Get the boy out of bed and get him dressed. You two are coming with me. Is there anyone else here in this house?" he demanded.

"No, no one. Go see for yourself," I suggested in very loud tones.

"What are you trying to do, Lady? Are you trying to warn someone?" he snapped.

"No, no, I'm just scared," I said as I broke into tears in an attempt to hide my real reason for yelling my answers.

I pulled jeans, socks, a shirt, and a jacket from Ryan's chest of drawers and closet. I helped him to dress and sat on the bed beside him as he put on his shoes and socks.

"You're already dressed. Why?" he asked me as he looked at me directly.

"I was sleeping on the sofa just in case you decided to break into my house. I didn't want to waste time trying to change from my night gown to blue jeans and a tee shirt," I said sarcastically. "I guess I was right about that."

"Get over here both of you. Stand in front of me and turn to your left as you walk out the door," he instructed as he viciously waved the gun.

I pushed Ryan in front of me and guided him by his shoulders to turn as we walked through the door.

The doors to Ellen and Emily's bedrooms were open, the beds were made, and it looked as if they had not been there at all.

"Who do these rooms belong to?" the gun wielding, masked man asked.

"My daughters, but they stayed the night with a friend," I said calmly. "I'm sure glad they decided to do that. I wish Ryan had done the same," I said as I pulled him closer to me.

Ryan glanced up at me with a questioning look.

"Is she telling the truth?" he asked Ryan.

Ryan nodded yes and then looked at the floor. That was his little sign that what he was saying was a complete and total fabrication.

"Cross the hall and open the door," he demanded.

I didn't want to open that door. Jed was on the other side and I didn't want this crazy man to find him and shoot him on sight.

I turned the knob, took a deep breath, and swung the door open slowly. All I could see was a rumpled bed, but no Jed.

"You said you were sleeping on the sofa. Who was sleeping in your bed?" he asked as he poked me with the gun.

"I was, but I couldn't hear what was going on outside so I just left it as it is and moved to the sofa in the living room," I said as I made the story up on the fly.

He looked over my shoulder at the unmade bed.

Where are Jed and the girls?

The closet doors in all three bedrooms had been open so he could see inside of them.

"Move on down the hall to the living room," he snarled.

Ryan and I shuffled our feet along the carpet. I had no idea what we thought we were doing, but shuffling our feet seemed to be right.

"Get moving!" he shouted. "Pick up your feet and move into the living room."

I pushed Ryan forward and we ran into the living room. This guy meant business and I decided we had better not antagonize him anymore.

"You two sit down on the sofa. I need to tie you up for a while," he said as he looked around the room, searching for something that he could use as rope.

He started to reach for the lamp cord when I said, "There is some rope in the kitchen under the sink. Please don't ruin my lamp," I begged. I was stalling for time. My gut was telling me that help was coming. I hoped one of my girls or Jed had dialed 9-1-1 for help. Jed was the only one who had a cell phone. I hoped one of them would have realized that was what they needed to do.

Suddenly a thought popped into my head.

Maybe the girls sneaked out the back door.

If they had, they wouldn't have been able to take Jed with them without making a lot of noise, considering the cast he had on his leg. Jed must still be in the house.

Why didn't I see Jed in the bedroom?

"You need to call your boyfriend," said the gunman.

"He's not my boyfriend. He is just a friend who needed help," I said sarcastically.

"I don't care, just call him," he snapped.

I didn't want to do that. I was afraid it would ring in the bedroom, because that was where he had had it.

"Call him, now," he said as he pushed the gun up into my face.

"Okay, let me have the phone," I said as I tried to push the gun away from my forehead.

I pushed the numbered buttons on the phone and waited. I didn't hear it ringing in the bedroom, so my thought was that he had turned the phone off.

"There is no answer. He must have it turned off for now," I said slowly, not sure of what kind a reaction I would get.

"Try again," he snarled.

Now I was getting really scared. I entered the phone number again into the keypad and prayed I would get an answer.

Jed's recorded greeting started running and I waited for it to finish.

"Jed, this is Lindsay. Call me right away. It's important," I said in a breathless whisper.

"He will call you back, won't he?" demanded the gunman.

"He always has," I answered. "Depending on what he is doing at the moment, he will get back to be as soon as he can."

I sat back on the sofa, pulled Ryan close to me in a weak effort to protect him, and closed my eyes for a moment. I had to get my thoughts back together. I had to figure out a way to get out of this mess.

I wanted so much to blame Jed for this whole incident, but I knew it wasn't his fault. At least, it wasn't completely his fault. Because of my stupid motherly instincts, I had known I had to help Jed, who had a broken and casted leg, to get on with his life for the next few days. Someone had to give him a hand and, of course, it had to be me.

"Call him again," the gunman said as he walked over to us and placed the gun against Ryan's head.

"Put that gun over here against my head," I shouted. "Don't hold it next to Ryan, please."

"Call him again and put it on speaker," he growled.

I picked up the phone and punched in the numbers. It rang three times and I thought it was going to the recorded message when I heard "Hello?"

"Is that you, Jed?" I asked when I didn't recognize the voice.

"Yeah, Lindsay?" asked the strange voice.

"Jed, there is a man here holding a gun on me and Ryan who wants to talk to you," I said as I thrust the phone at the gunman, catching him off guard.

"Are you Jed?" asked the impatient gunman.

"Yes, what do you want?" asked the strange voice.

"Do you want to see your girlfriend again?" the gunman snarled.

"Yes, of course I do. What do you want?" asked the strange voice.

"I need you tell me what you found out about the Martin family. I especially want to know where they can be found," said the gunman.

"Nobody told me anything. The people I talked to don't have any idea where they are, just that they're on vacation. That's what they were told and that's what they told me," said the strange voice.

"That's not good enough," he said as he shook the gun in my face again.

"I can try to find out. Why do you need to find them?" asked the strange voice in a conversational tone.

"It's a contractual obligation that I have to fulfill for the organization I work for," he said in language I wouldn't have expected to come out of the mouth of a hired gunman.

"What does that mean? Are you planning to kill them?" demanded the strange voice.

"If they aren't dead already," the gunman responded.

I heard a noise coming from outside. I couldn't tell what it was. I pulled Ryan closer to me again.

The gunman turned his head toward the sound and I leaned forward, grabbing his leg and yanking with all of my might.

The gun went in the air and landed on the sofa next to me. I picked it up and shot it in the air. I wanted to get the attention of anyone who might be outside.

My front door burst open and what looked like a platoon of uniformed policemen swarmed into my tiny living room. They knocked the gunman to the floor and had him handcuffed in a matter of seconds.

I held Ryan close to me and went searching for all of the missing people: Ellen, Emily, and Jed.

I ran into the hallway and shouted each name as loudly as I could.

I heard the clump, clump sound of Jed coming out of my bedroom.

"Where were you hiding? You couldn't have been in the bedroom all of this time. We would have seen you when we looked inside the room," I said.

"I was on the other side of the bed. If you had walked in a little further, you would have seen me. I was crunched up under the far side of the bed. I went as far as I could crawl with the cast on my leg. That's where I called the police after I motioned for the girls to run out the back door," he said as he hugged me and Ryan.

"Where are they now? Ellen and Emily, I mean," I asked as I looked around, searching for them.

"They are right here," said a policeman as he led the girls to me. I grabbed onto to both of them and held on for dear life.

"How did you get someone to answer your phone in Bristol?" I asked.

"It was a neighbor who I got a hold of and whispered the story to from the bedroom. I must say, it is hard to keep a full conversation going with someone on the telephone when you are afraid someone will hear you in the other room," he said as he grinned.

"Why did all of this happen?" I asked no one in particular. I just wanted someone to answer me.

"This is a result of a drug deal gone bad," said Everett as he walked into the room. "The Martins were present when the deal was made and knew all of the people involved in the transaction. They testified against all of the people who were present when the deal was made and the major players in the drug network weren't happy about it. The Martins were marked for death."

"Are the Martins dead?" I asked, thinking of Annie and her neighbor.

"Unfortunately, they are. We found their bodies two days ago. They had been dumped off of a ridge up in the mountains. We were trying to keep Dennis Martin alive, but that, too, was becoming difficult," answered Detective Sims, who was standing near Everett.

"Was Dennis Martin a witness?" I asked.

"Dennis Martin knows nothing about the drug deal. He was a little boy when all of this happened," answered Everett.

"What will Dennis Martin do now?" I asked.

"I don't know yet. All he wants to do is keep his house and stay in this town. I think he has a girlfriend who he wants to get to know a little better," said Everett with a knowing smile.

"Do you think it will be safe?" I asked.

"Yes, it should be known to all the important people participating in this hit scheme that Dennis Martin knows nothing that could be used against them," said the detective as Everett nodded his head in agreement.

"What happens now?" I asked the detective.

"You all need a place to stay for a couple of nights while this crime scene is checked out. I am Detective Sims. Give me a call when you get settled and we will let you know what the next step is going to be. If it goes to trial, you will have to testify. If he pleads guilty, there won't be a trial ahead of you and it will all be over," said the detective.

"Let's all get in the car and go to my house. It will be crowded, but we can make an adventure out of it," Jed said as he tried to gather all of us close.

"Mom, what can we do to help Maddie?" asked Emily.

"She will be my next project. Okay Emily?"

Emily nodded her head in agreement.

"All I was trying to do when this all started was find out who killed Annie's dog. Detective, can you tell me who killed my friend Annie's dog? She is Dennis Martin's neighbor," I asked.

"I believe it was the man we arrested. There was a prowler reported around the Martin house a couple of times. He probably poisoned the dog to shut him up," said the detective.

"Well, that only proves that SNOOPING CAN BE DOGGONE DEADLY," I said with a laugh.

ABOUT THE AUTHOR

Linda Hudson Hoagland of Tazewell, Virginia, graduate of Southwest Virginia Community College, has won acclaim for her novels, short stories, essays, and poems. Many of her works have been published in anthologies such as *Cup of Comfort* along with the publication of her ten mystery novels, six nonfiction books, a collection of short stories and a volume of poetry.

Awards

2014 – Green River Writers Flash Fiction Contest
Third Place – *Nancy's Reality*

2014 – Sherwood Anderson Short Story Contest
First Place – Short Story Contest – *The Noise*

2014 – On the Same Page Literary Award
Second Place Non-Fiction – *His Red Headed Wife*

2014 – Alabama Writers Conclave
Third Place – Creative Nonfiction – *Pick It Up, Please*

2014 – Alabama Writers Conclave
Fourth Place – Short Story – *November 4th*

2014 – The Writers' Workshop
Honorable Mention – Hard Times Contest – *Starting Over–Again*

2013 – *The Storyteller Magazine* – People's Choice Award for Poetry
Third Place – *Politicians*

2013 – Chautauqua Creative Writing Contest
Honorable Mention – Adult Essay

2012 – Dream Quest One
First Writing Prize – *I Am Mom*

2012 – Virginia Writers Club
Second Place – *No Service*

2012 – Westmoreland Arts & Heritage Festival
Honorable Mention – *Welcome to Whistler*

2012 – Tennessee Mountain Writers
Second Place – *And the Next Day...*

2012 – The Seacoast Writers Association
Third Place – *Getting Myself Primed*

2012 – West Virginia Writers
Honorable Mention – *I'm Not Ready*

2011 – Women's Memoirs – All Things Labor
Honorable Mention – *Penance*

2011 – Alabama Writers Conclave
Honorable Mention – First Chapter of a Novel – *Writing the Circuit*

2011 – Alabama Writers Conclave
Juvenile Fiction – *The Lady in the Sun*

2011 – Appalachian Heritage Writers Symposium
Second Place – Adult Essay – *Surprise Package*

2011 – Writers-Editors Network International Writing Competition
Honorable Mention – Nonfiction – *Getting Myself Primed*

2011 – Tennessee Mountain Writers
Writing for Young People – *I Dare You*

2010 – The Jesse Stuart Prize for Young Adult Writing
Second Place – *How's That For Real*

2010 – Tampa Writers Alliance – Novel
Honorable Mention – *Quilt Pieces*

2010 – Alabama Writers Conclave – Nonfiction
Third Prize – *Four Large Eggs*

2008 – Nominee Governor's Award for the Arts

2007 – Sherwood Anderson Short Story Contest
First Place – Category V

Many other awards have not been listed.

Coming Soon

Lindsay delves into the life of
Maddie Stevens, a homeless teenager in
SNOOPING CAN BE HELPFUL